A hand over her mouth awakened her. . . .

"Don't scream."

Hawk! Her eyes adjusted to the darkness. He was bending over her, dressed in the same buckskin shirt and jeans he'd worn to the rally. The hilt of his knife gleamed in the darkness.

She reached for him, and his mouth slammed down on hers. They kissed without restraint and without mercy, as if he had just returned from war. The kiss went on and on until she was dizzy for lack of air.

At last he lifted his head. "I didn't mean to come back, Elizabeth."

"I know."

"I couldn't stay away. Not after seeing you again."

"I'm glad." She reached for the lacings on his shirt and began to pull them apart. Then she plunged her hand into the opening and pressed it flat on his chest. She could feel the hammering of his heart.

"I came through the tunnel so no one would see," he said.

"Right now I don't care if the whole world sees," she replied.

"I won't endanger you, Elizabeth."

"Shhh." She put her hand over his mouth. "Don't talk. I don't want to waste a moment of our time together talking."

He pulled her tight against him. "You're mine. . . ."

WHAT ARE *LOVESWEPT* ROMANCES?

They are stories of true romance and touching emotion. We believe those two very important ingredients are constants in our highly sensual and very believable stories in the *LOVESWEPT* line. Our goal is to give you, the reader, stories of consistently high quality that may sometimes make you laugh, sometimes make you cry, but are always fresh and creative and contain many delightful surprises within their pages.

Most romance fans read an enormous number of books. Those they truly love, they keep. Others may be traded with friends and soon forgotten. We hope that each *LOVESWEPT* romance will be a treasure—a "keeper." We will always try to publish

LOVE STORIES YOU'LL NEVER FORGET
BY AUTHORS YOU'LL ALWAYS REMEMBER

The Editors

Peggy Webb

The Secret Life of Elizabeth McCade

BANTAM BOOKS
NEW YORK · TORONTO · LONDON · SYDNEY · AUCKLAND

THE SECRET LIFE OF ELIZABETH McCADE
A Bantam Book / October 1991

*If you would be interested in receiving protective vinyl
covers for your Loveswept books, please write to this address
for information:*

> *Loveswept
> Bantam Books
> P.O. Box 985
> Hicksville, NY 11802*

ISBN 0-553-44191-4

Published simultaneously in the United States and Canada

*Bantam Books are published by Bantam Books, a division
of Bantam Doubleday Dell Publishing Group, Inc. Its trademark, consisting of the words "Bantam Books" and the
portrayal of a rooster, is Registered in U.S. Patent and
Trademark Office and in other countries. Marca Registrada.
Bantam Books, 666 Fifth Avenue, New York, New York
10103.*

This book is dedicated to Governor Bill Anoatubby, his wonderful staff, and all the proud people of the Chickasaw Nation.

Author's Note: Before the Treaty of Pontotoc in 1832, Mississippi was one of the homelands of the Chickasaw Nation. After that treaty and the subsequent Treaty of Doaksville in 1837, the Chickasaw Nation relocated to Oklahoma. The present seat of tribal government is Ada, Oklahoma. For purposes of this story, I have taken literary license with history and left this proud nation in its Mississippi homeland.

I gratefully acknowledge the help of Governor Bill Anoatubby and his staff in providing a history of the Chickasaw Nation. Any mistakes I have made in the portrayal of the Chickasaws are entirely my own.

The Secret Life of Elizabeth McCade

Prologue

Black Hawk stood high on the ridge overlooking Tombigbee Bluff. The lights of the city beamed serenely into the night. On the outskirts of town, Tombigbee Forest was so silent, it appeared to be sleeping. Not a breeze stirred the pine boughs; not a sound gave away nature's creatures, busy with their nocturnal errands. It might have been any other summer night in Mississippi.

Black Hawk knew better. Straining his eyes into the darkness, he saw the silent line of Chickasaws, *his people*, ringing the forest three deep, keeping watch over their ancestral lands. When morning came, the Chickasaws would be facing a line of equally determined white men, the politicians and developers of Tombigbee Bluff, intent upon turning a portion of tribal land into a shopping mall.

His people had held the barricade for two months, deadlocked with the city fathers. Tempers were high, and patience was running thin. Isolated incidents of violence destroyed a chance of a peaceful settlement. Blood had already been shed . . . and there would be more.

Black Hawk left the ridge. His watch was over. It

was time to go back through the forest and beyond the vast reaches of the Chickasaw tribal lands to his ranch. His stallion was waiting for him at the foot of the ridge.

He vaulted onto the horse's back and set a swift course toward home. The trees whispered primeval secrets in his ears, and a lonely nighthawk soared above him in graceful splendor. In time, he reached the clearing that bordered his ranch.

With silent signals he drew his horse to a stop. Lifting his head, Black Hawk inhaled the subtle fragrances of the land—the fecund smells of the rich, black earth, the pungent scent of pine, the heady sweetness of honeysuckle. Suddenly he stiffened. There was another smell in the air, a smell that didn't belong there—smoke.

Digging his heels into the stallion's sides, he galloped toward his house. Sirens wailed in the distance.

Racing now, his heart riding high in his chest, he rounded a copse of trees and saw his house. It was blanketed in flames. Emergency vehicles ringed his yard, red lights blinking.

Black Hawk drew his stallion to a standstill and studied the scene. Last week his car had been firebombed, and this week his house. The enemy wanted Black Hawk dead.

Flames leaped toward the sky, crackling with a voice of evil intent. He urged his horse forward, stopping only when he was even with Sheriff Wayne Blodgett's car. The sheriff got out and came slowly toward Black Hawk, huffing under an excess of fifty pounds and wiping sweat from his face.

"It's hotter than a witch's caldron out here tonight," he said, moving the handkerchief around his beefy neck and into the collar of his chambray shirt. When he reached Black Hawk, he caught the stallion's bridle. "Good evenin', Blackie."

"Is it?" Black Hawk stared at his house. Nothing would be saved: It was too late.

"I'm damned sorry. You know that." Wayne wiped at his face once more. "It's that thing with the mall developers. They're after your blood."

"Why?"

"You know damned well why. You're the leader of the resistance. If it hadn't been for you, this whole thing would have been over six weeks ago."

"And a vast section of trees would be destroyed to make way for another ugly concrete mall—the white man's monument to civilization." Black Hawk dismounted, then bent down and picked up a piece of charred debris that had separated from the burning mass of his house. Clutching the board in his hand, he stood up, facing his friend.

"I'll die before I'll give up one tree on my ancestral lands."

Sheriff Blodgett swore until his face was only a shade lighter than the fire that roared in the background. Then he put his hand on Black Hawk's shoulder.

"That's exactly what they want, Blackie: They want you dead." Black Hawk was silent, watching his friend with eyes as dark as the night sky. Wayne pulled a piece of paper from his pocket. It was torn and dingy. "Read this."

Black Hawk held the paper up to catch the light from the flames. "You're next, Indian. Pull that renegade band of yours back from the forest or you die."

"Where did you get this?"

Wayne spat onto the ground. "Found it stuck with an arrow in that oak tree over yonder."

"I won't be intimidated." Black Hawk handed the paper back to the sheriff. "Check that out. Work with the Tombigbee Bluff police—if they aren't already in the pockets of the developers."

"I want you to get out of town, Blackie. Lay low for a while."

"No. I stay."

"Dammit all. There's been enough violence.

"Nobody has been killed. It won't come to that. The developers won't go that far."

"I don't know that and neither do you." Wayne stuffed the paper into his back pocket. "I can't protect you, Black Hawk. I don't have the resources."

"I will protect myself." He clapped his hand on his friend's shoulder. "We've offered to negotiate with the city and the developers for a peaceful settlement. This will all be over soon."

"I hope you're right, Blackie . . . or else somebody is liable to get killed."

"You worry too much, old friend."

Black Hawk's foreman and all the ranch hands, drawn out of bed by the commotion, joined the vigil beside the blaze. The fire fight continued into the night, and at last only Black Hawk and Wayne were left beside the rubble that had once been a home.

"Come home with me tonight, Blackie. Jane will be glad to have you, and you know how the kids feel about you. They think you're some damned hero."

"Thanks, friend, but I'll stay here. Somebody might come back to see how well they did their job."

"Be careful."

Wayne's parting warning was still echoing in Black Hawk's mind when he got a saddle blanket from the barn and spread his bed under the stars. Being careful was not his style. Boldness and passion ruled Black Hawk, ruled him to the extent that his family and all his friends declared he was a ticking time bomb waiting to explode.

He could feel the passion for battle rising within him. Let the enemy come. He was ready.

The enemy came out of the night, using a white man's stealth. Black Hawk lay flat on the ground, hidden by a scrub of pines, waiting and smiling. He had heard their approach fifteen minutes earlier. They were about as stealthy as a herd of runaway buffalo.

The men filed into the clearing. There were ten of them, all milling around his burned-out house, looking for signs of him. Black Hawk recognized four of them; they were the most belligerent of the mall supporters, the troublemakers, the ones always ready to fight rather than to talk.

Well, he was more than ready to talk; he was eager. He wanted answers. He rose from his spying place with the intention of joining the enemy, when he spotted the glint of a gun barrel. He froze, studying the situation. Walter Martin, standing on the fringe of the crowd, was holding a Winchester rifle. One man with a gun could incite an unarmed mob to riot. It would be ten against one. Though walking away was not his style, Black Hawk had no intention of starting a war—or of being an easy target.

He raced toward the wood, going away from his men and his property, his moccasins silent on the spongy forest floor. He'd been running only a few minutes when he heard the mob thrashing along behind him.

"We'll never catch that Indian if we don't spread out," one of them yelled.

Black Hawk stripped his shirt off and left it on a bush to confuse them.

Behind him, he heard the commotion as the mob tried to figure out which way he had gone. Black Hawk followed a small stream north until it forked, racing into the night.

Suddenly there was a yell from the thicket on Black Hawk's right.

"I got him."

He felt the sting as a bullet pierced his right arm. Black Hawk hunched low, clutching his arm. He could shoot well enough to part a man's hair without harming his scalp, even with the blood warm on his own skin. But he didn't want to resort to their brand of negotiation. If he couldn't scare his enemies out of the woods, he would wait them out.

Taking his knife, he cut through the thicket of vines and brambles. All at once, the earth opened up and swallowed him. He rolled himself into a ball, tumbling downward for a small eternity. Jutting stones and sharp roots pierced him.

He was still conscious when he landed. The yelling of the mob seemed to come from a long way off.

One

There was blood on her kitchen floor.

Elizabeth McCade knelt in her business suit and high-heel shoes to investigate. In the light from the fluorescent bulbs, the spot glowed darkly against the tiles.

"It can't possibly be blood," she said matter-of-factly. "I'm so tired from working such late hours, my mind is playing tricks."

Nevertheless she dipped one finger into the spot and inspected it carefully. A shiver ran through her. The red substance was definitely blood.

Elizabeth stood up quietly and carefully, drawing her suit jacket around her as if the ancient air conditioner in her kitchen window was suddenly blasting arctic air. She pulled off her shoes and walked in stocking feet to the pantry where she kept a flashlight. The most logical place for an intruder to hide was the cellar, and the lights had long since burned out down there. Arming herself, she started toward the cellar, then changed her mind and searched the rest of her house first.

Outside her windows the wind picked up, moaning around the gables and whistling through the lattices. Elizabeth wasn't easily spooked, but then she wasn't accustomed to coming home at two o'clock in the morning and finding blood on her kitchen floor.

After a search of her first and second floors, she pushed open the door that led into the wine cellar, training her flashlight into the darkness.

Deep in the shadows, Black Hawk heard the door open, heard the footsteps on the stairs. He surveyed his surroundings, looking for hiding places. There were none . . . except the wine racks. Fortunately they were the massive kind favored by the wealthy in the early nineteenth century, built solidly of red oak. Swiftly and silently he climbed a wine rack and flattened himself along the top. One bottle threatened to topple. He caught it with his right hand and eased it back into place, gritting his teeth against the pain.

The searcher, with steps as quiet as cat feet, traversed the basement, and played the light along the floor and the walls. Black Hawk held his breath, praying whomever it was didn't point the beam upward.

"Is anybody here?"

The searcher was a woman.

"Come out with your hands raised. I have a gun, and I know how to use it."

In spite of his situation, Black Hawk was amused. The woman was as spunky as hell. He eased his head over the side of the wine rack and looked down. In the glow of the flashlight he saw her. She had gleaming black hair, and her face radiated intelligence and passion—and she was holding a nickel-plated .44 Magnum pistol with an eight-inch barrel.

Black Hawk added *tough* to his list of her assets.

The woman stood for a while, holding the gun steady, searching the cellar once more with her beam of light. "It must have been that stray cat," she said, then turned and went back up the stairs.

Black Hawk waited atop the wine rack until he considered it safe to come down. His body was bloody and battered, and he ached with each movement he made.

What had tipped the woman off? He had been careful on his foraging expedition upstairs. He had found bandages and antiseptic salve and had taken them without guilt, guessing they would never be missed. He had drunk his fill of water, then washed the glass and put it back in its place. Food was not a problem yet. He intended to wait until the next day to decide how much he could take without arousing her suspicions.

Moving slowly because of his injuries, Black Hawk made himself as comfortable as possible on a couple of burlap bags he'd found, and took stock of his situation. He still had his gun and his knife. He'd sacrificed his shirt to throw the enemy off his trail, but he had his pants and his moccasins. The gunshot wound in his right arm was painful but not serious. The bullet had passed through, grazing the skin. Most of the cuts and bruises he'd suffered during the plunge into the passageway were on his chest and arms.

Black Hawk would be recovered enough to leave in a few days. In the meantime, he needed to check out his unsuspecting hostess. If she was as lethal as her gun, then he had stumbled onto a dangerous hiding place. Were the gods watching over him when he had plunged into the hole and discovered a decaying passageway that led to this wine cellar, or were they mocking him?

With a patience as ancient as time itself, Black Hawk waited until the house was still. The gurgling water pipes and creaking floorboards had long since grown quiet.

Armed with his knife, Black Hawk stole up the stairs and into the kitchen. He stood long enough to let his eyes adjust, then he followed the trail of the woman. She was not hard to follow; her scent lingered in the air, a faint, musky fragrance that made him think of exotic dancers wearing nothing but veils. That thought led him to another: He hadn't made love with a woman in a long time. Soon he would have to remedy that. His appetite for women was as big as his appetite for danger; and he appeased both of them often.

He found her upstairs. She lay stretched across her bed, asleep on her stomach. The black hair he had glimpsed in the cellar was unpinned and hung down her back like a bolt of silk. A red satin gown outlined shapely legs, trim hips, and a slim waist. Her body had been made for a man.

Black Hawk approached the bed, standing so close, he could have touched her silk-clad thighs. Ancient urgings stirred his loins and threatened the tempo of his breathing. He forced himself back under control.

He stood over the bed, watching her, assessing her, then turned away and quietly began to search her belongings. On his first trip upstairs he had been after the bare necessities: medicine and water. Now he wanted answers.

He found them in her closet and in her desk. She was a paradox: a woman with the soul of a wanton, posing as an archconservative. Her business suits were plain, even severe; but her lingerie ran the gamut from seductive to outrageously naughty.

She was Elizabeth McCade, a loan officer at the local bank, twenty-seven-year-old daughter of Lonnie and Regina McCade, born in Tombigbee Bluff and educated at Yale. She had a degree in English, a teaching certificate, and a locked diary.

Black Hawk put her personal papers back into

her desk and returned to the bed. Elizabeth Mc-Cade had not stirred.

He bent over and traced the curve of her hip with one finger. "Who are you, Elizabeth McCade?" he whispered. "Woman of ice or woman of fire?"

Her fragrance wafted over him, and he inhaled deeply. Another time, another place he would have enjoyed getting to know her. But now his passion was for destroying his enemies.

He left her bedroom and went back to his hiding place in the wine cellar.

Elizabeth was missing a piece of cheese and a small amount of milk. She knew the food was gone because only that morning before she had left for the bank, she had taken stock in order to prepare her grocery list.

The day before, the blood, and now the food. She could no longer blame the stray cat. Cats couldn't open refrigerators.

The first thing she did was go to her pantry and get her .44 Magnum. Then she sat at her kitchen table and decided what to do. It was already dark outside. Sheriff Wayne Blodgett wouldn't be in his office, and she was reluctant to call him at home on such flimsy evidence. After all, she *could* be mistaken about the food. But not the blood. There was still a small stain in the grout around the tile. She was going to have to buy a special cleaning product to remove it.

She could rule out drop-in friends and nosey neighbors. Her nearest neighbor was two miles away, and her friends were not the drop-in kind. Since coming home to Mississippi, Elizabeth had discouraged anyone who'd tried to get too close. The people who came into her home were *invited*—or had been until the day before. Apparently there was an uninvited guest in her home, and she intended to route him out.

Picking up her pistol, she made another careful inspection of her house, starting with the second floor. She had her head in the bedroom closet when her phone rang. Elizabeth kept up her search. She was not expecting a business call, and she was in no mood for a social call.

Her answering machine kicked in. "Elizabeth, this is Kenneth . . . Kenneth Spain . . . the guy who has been calling you for the last three weeks." Elizabeth felt her temper rising. Didn't that man ever give up?

He continued his pitch, his voice amplified by the receiver. "Listen, I know all the stories about you, but I don't believe any of them. I think you're just waiting for the right guy . . . and I'm the perfect one. Call me."

Elizabeth would not return his call, just as she hadn't returned the call of the half dozen other men who had pursued her the last few months. Summer seemed to bring out the beast in men. But it wouldn't bring out the beast in her. Of that she was absolutely certain.

The search for an intruder proved futile in the main part of the house. That left the wine cellar. Gripping her gun and her flashlight, Elizabeth started down the staircase, taking the bold approach.

"I know you're down here, and I intend to find you." Standing on the second step from the bottom, she shined the light around the cellar. She saw nothing except dust, cobwebs, a mouse, and the wine racks holding bottles dating from the time her parents had occupied the house.

"I'm holding a gun and I'm a deadly shot." She waited, listening. There was no sound, but she had the eerie feeling that she was not alone.

Prickles of awareness danced along the back of her neck.

"I'm going to give you to the count of ten to come out. After that, I start shooting." She was bluffing. The bullets would ricochet on the concrete walls, but she hoped the intruder wouldn't know that. She laid the flashlight on the bottom steps, pointing the beam into the darkness, then got into a shooting stance, holding on to her gun with both hands.

"One . . . two . . . three . . ."

The arm hooked around her from behind. A hot hand clamped over her mouth, and the cold steel of a knife blade rested against her throat.

"Don't shoot, Elizabeth McCade, or you might get both of us killed."

Even though she was holding a gun, she knew her throat would be slit before the bullet had found its mark. She forced herself to breathe normally and to stand perfectly still. She didn't want to give the stranger any excuse to use his knife.

"I'm not going to hurt you unless you create a commotion."

That qualified as good news. The bad news was that he knew her name. She had read that most violent acts occurred between people who knew each other. Fear rose up in her. She knew she would be helpless if she didn't bring it under control.

"I'm going to take my hand off your mouth now and take your gun. Don't try to turn around and don't make a sound, or you'll be dead."

The knife blade inched away from her throat, and she nodded her head slightly to show she understood. His hot hand left her mouth and took her gun.

"That's good, Elizabeth McCade. You're a smart woman."

Her captor had one of the richest, most melodic voices she'd ever heard. Her fear began to abate, and anger took its place. A criminal had no business with a voice like that. It could be a powerful weapon against the unsuspecting.

"What do you want?" she asked, surprised that her own voice was strong and controlled.

"I must stay here for a few days, and you must tell no one."

"Why?"

She started to turn around, but he pressed the knife blade against her throat again.

"Don't," he said.

"Who are you?"

"I'm not a criminal."

"How do you know my name?"

"I studied your personal belongings last night while you slept."

"You came into my bedroom?"

"Yes. Your hair was spread across the pillow, and you were wearing red. I was tempted to take more than your personal belongings."

A shiver ran through Elizabeth. She was suddenly aware of the man's body, of his muscular arms around her shoulders, of his broad chest bracing her back, of his hard legs pressing against hers. He was tall and solidly built. If it came to a test between his strength and hers, she would be the loser. Nevertheless, she couldn't contain her fury.

"You had no right to invade my privacy. This is *my* home. This is *my* sanctuary." Anger made her struggle against him.

"Don't move, Elizabeth." Suddenly the knife was withdrawn from her throat. There was small movement behind her back, then the stranger's hands were in her hair. Her hairpins fell to the concrete floor, and her heavy hair unfolded.

She felt his hands caressing, lifting, smoothing her hair. *Stop that,* she wanted to scream. But she dared not push him too far. He had said he was not a criminal, but he hadn't identified himself, and she had no reason to believe him.

"Who are you?" she asked once more.

He didn't answer. Instead his hands played through her hair for a small eternity.

"Your hair smells like the rest of you, exotic and mysterious." His hot breath seared the back of her neck. "Are you exotic and mysterious, Elizabeth?"

"Not nearly as mysterious as you." There was a strange, mesmerizing power about this invader. She felt almost as if she knew him, as if they knew each other. "Who are you?"

There was a long, dark silence. The sounds of their harsh breathing mingled, giving the cellar a sense of hushed expectancy. Elizabeth called on all her resources to be strong against the man who had invaded her home. Sweat dampened her palms and popped out on her brow.

"I am Black Hawk, and I seek refuge with you for a few days."

Slowly she turned around. Black Hawk. He was the leader of the Chickasaw resistance to progress without conscience, owner of one of the largest cattle ranches in Mississippi, both a hero and a target of the press, a man of mystery and danger and intrigue, and he was standing in her cellar injured and bleeding. His strong, fierce face had graced many a front page of the newspaper, and his voice had thundered from the late-night television news shows in defense of his Chickasaw nation.

She knew him—not as a person, but as a symbol of all that was brave and fearless. He was a crusader, a man out to preserve the dignity of the world he lived in.

In the feeble glow of her flashlight she saw a crude bandage on his upper right arm, and angry scratches and bruises on his chest and arms. No longer afraid or angry, she reached out and put her hand on his forehead. He stared silently at her with eyes as black as night.

"You have a fever," she said. She supposed the fever accounted for his hot hands, although seeing him now, even dimly, she knew he was the kind of man whose hands would be that hot with passion. *One kindred soul recognizes another.*

Seeing him, touching him, her passion kindled quickly and without restraint. Hard on its heels came astonishment. Not since Mark Laton had a man caused such a tumultuous physical response in her. And Mark Laton had nearly destroyed her.

Oh, God, she silently prayed. *Don't let it happen again.* Black Hawk watched her with searching dark eyes. She had the crazy sensation that he was reaching out and touching her skin. She nearly groaned aloud. This man had danger written all over him. If Mark had been a henchman from hell, Black Hawk was the very devil himself.

Elizabeth bit her lip until she tasted blood. The small jolt of pain kept her from reaching out to the man who had the potential to be her partner, her captor, her slave.

"Come with me." She turned her back on him in order to release herself from his spell.

"Where?"

"Upstairs. I have a bedroom."

"Yours?"

An image of him in her bed, his bronze body gracing her sheets and his black eyes searing her soul, made her knees weak. She resisted her darker impulses.

"Not mine." She faced him once more. "I have a

small spare bedroom on the first floor. I'll take care of you."

"I must not be seen. Your life as well as mine could be jeopardized."

"Don't worry. I live apart." When he made no comment, she added, "I'm not antisocial, but no one comes here without an invitation. We will be alone."

He smiled then. "Captivity has its rewards."

"Who is the captive? You or me?"

He took her hand and led her to the bedroom.

"Both of us."

Two

Black Hawk didn't release her hand at the top of the stairs, and Elizabeth didn't try to pull away. Although he shouldn't have known where her spare bedroom was located, he led her right to it.

She supposed he had either explored her entire house, or she was communicating with him by ESP and body language. And was her body ever speaking a language! Her breasts were peaked and hardened, straining against her silk blouse like wild things trying to get free. Her limbs felt slack, and a heat centered in her lower body was slowly building and spreading. For a moment she thought she was back at Yale, holding on to the hand of Dr. Mark Laton, heading to the small cot in his office in the musty old building where he taught Chaucer.

She slid her glance sideways at her captor. He was nothing like Mark. Mark had been a small man, blond and compactly built. Black Hawk was lean and angular with looks that bordered on handsome but could have been called rugged and untamed.

"Draw the curtains," he said suddenly, stopping outside the bedroom door.

Elizabeth walked swiftly across the bedroom and drew the heavy curtains. Then she snapped on a small lamp on the bedside table. Its feeble glow illuminated an iron bedstead, spread with a simple white comforter.

Black Hawk came into the circle of light and stood looking down at the bed. Elizabeth scarcely breathed. What was happening to her? Fires of passion raged through her, fires she had kept under control for the last seven years.

Black Hawk turned his head and stared at her. Not even Mark Laton, with his silver tongue and his skilled hands, had made her feel the way this strange savage warrior did. She had spent seven years running not only from Mark but from her own passions. Suddenly, she was face-to-face with her past. She held her breath so long, the room started to spin. When she thought she might faint, he spoke.

"Have you slept here, Elizabeth?"

"Yes."

"Good. My body will lie where yours has been." He turned his back to her and began to strip off his jeans.

She watched him with unabashed pleasure. His body was a work of art. When he had rid himself of every stitch of clothing, he turned to face her.

"Now you may care for me, Elizabeth."

She stood still, her gaze roaming over him. He was totally without shame, an Adam to her Eve. He was neither embarrassed nor self-conscious nor arrogant in his nakedness.

She couldn't speak. She doubted that she even could move.

"I desire a cool hand upon my body, Elizabeth."

Elizabeth dared not show her vulnerability. She dared not show this self-contained, inscrutable man that the thing she wanted most was to take him into her bed and do his bidding. Oh, Lord! Would her past never die? Would she never be able to make her body forget?

Steeling herself against his sensual assault, she strode to the bed and ripped back the covers. When the sheet was exposed, she turned to Black Hawk.

"Lie down."

He stretched upon the sheets, a tall man who made the bed look small. "I'm yours, Elizabeth. Do with me as you will."

Was he reading her mind? If she did what she wanted, she would start at his neck and caress her way down his body.

"The first thing you need is to have your wounds cleaned," she said, striding briskly toward the small adjoining bathroom.

Inside the bathroom, she shut the door and leaned over the lavatory. She thought she was going to be sick. Her stomach was churning, and her chest felt as if a huge weight were pressing against it. Lifting her head, she drew several deep breaths. In the mirror, her face was as pale as death.

"Damn you, Black Hawk," she whispered. "You're just another man."

She brought herself under sharp control, then set about doing what she must. Her sympathies had long lain with Black Hawk as she had followed the news stories about him. He was right about progress. Progress was *not* raping the land with no thought for the past or the future. Progress was a harmonious blending of the past with the present, of man with nature.

She would give him refuge. She would bind his wounds and give him food, drink, and shelter. And when he was ready to face the enemy, she would let him go and forget about him. It would only be a few days, no more. Surely she could control the dark side of her nature for a few days.

Armed with towels, washcloths, a bottle of peroxide, and a basin of warm water, she went back into the bedroom. Black Hawk hadn't moved a muscle. He was as still as a bronze carving . . . and just as beautiful.

She hesitated in the doorway, admiring him. Slowly he turned his head and looked at her. Passion crackled in the stillness.

"Do you have what you need?" he finally asked.

"Yes."

"Then come." He held out his hand. "Touch me."

She came to his bed and bent quickly over him, leaning so that her hair made a curtain that shielded his lower body. She wasn't about to draw the sheet over him. Not by word or sign would she betray her feelings.

"You need not make this sound so erotic. It's strictly clinical." He didn't flinch as she started rubbing at the angry gash across his chest.

"Do my words sound erotic to you, Elizabeth?"

She didn't answer, didn't look at his face. He lay perfectly still as she worked. Every time her breathing threatened to become shallow, she bit down hard on her lower lip. Tomorrow it would be bruised, maybe even swollen. She couldn't help that. It was a small price to pay for sanity.

As she cleaned his chest and arms, she tried to keep the washcloth as a shield between her flesh and his. It was impossible. Occasionally her fingers glided along his skin. It was remarkably satiny, with hard muscles just beneath the surface.

Caught in a time warp, she closed her eyes and swayed. She was going under, drowning in sensation.

"I love your hands upon me." Her eyes snapped

open. Black Hawk was looking at her with the dark knowledge of a sorcerer. He caught her wrist and pressed her palm flat across his heart. "Feel how my heart races."

"Please," she whispered.

"You have learned hands, Elizabeth."

She jerked herself free. Touching him was more than foolish: It was dangerous.

"I think you can finish this job. Clean linens and medical supplies are in the bathroom closet. Use this peroxide on your wounds before you bind them."

She stood up and headed for the door. He didn't speak until she was almost there.

"Elizabeth." His voice compelled her to turn around. He was sitting up with the sheet draped over his hips and the hilt of his knife showing underneath his pillow. She hadn't even heard him move.

"You must cleanse the wounds on my back."

"There is a small shower in the bathroom," she said, holding on to the doorknob. "That should be sufficient."

"No. I need you."

His voice was as quiet as storm clouds gathering over the desert, and just as deadly. She was swept away in a flood tide of emotions. His eyes commanded her, and she obeyed, moving back toward his bed as if she were in a dream.

When she was standing over him, their gazes clashed, dark eyes warring with dark eyes. She balled her hands into fists, squeezing so hard, her fingernails bit into her palms.

"Lie on your stomach," she said.

He reached out and traced the contours of her cheek, then turned onto his stomach. She drew her breath at the sight of his back. It was bruised and lacerated. Bending down, she tenderly touched the wounds. He didn't flinch.

"Do they hurt?"

"Pain is a matter of perspective. All the wounds on my back don't pain me nearly as much as the thought of the destruction of my ancestral lands. I must recover quickly in order to fight."

"I'll help you." She worked silently and swiftly, unaware that she made small humming sounds as her hands moved over his body.

Black Hawk lay very still, reveling in her touch and the sound of her voice. Whether the sounds she made were of pleasure or of succor, he didn't know. All he knew was that he had to have the woman bending over him. Soon . . . soon he would have her. But first, he had to rest, had to close his eyes for just a moment.

"I'll bring you some soup . . . and aspirin. You are burning with fever."

Her voice faded away. Black Hawk fought for consciousness, struggled to stay awake so he would know every place she touched, remember every silken caress of her cool hands.

Elizabeth bandaged his wounds and straightened up. "I'm finished." He didn't stir. She touched his shoulder. "Black Hawk?" He was sound asleep.

"Rest well." She tiptoed from the room and sat down at her kitchen table. He needed sleep. Food and aspirin could wait a while. In the meantime, she was going to prepare herself for battle . . . against his enemy and against her own private demons.

The first thing she did was go back into the basement to retrieve her gun. It lay on the concrete floor beside Black Hawk's rifle.

"Quite an arsenal you have here, Elizabeth Mc-Cade." Smiling grimly, she collected the weapons and marched up the stairs. Standing against his enemy was going to be no problem, but it was going to take more than an arsenal to hold firm against her own.

Throughout the early part of the night, Black Hawk was haunted by visions. He saw flames that leaped into the sky, crackling with fury, consuming his house. Then the flames became a glimpse of red satin, whispering erotic promises, brushing against his skin. Dreams blended with reality so that he struggled to know the difference.

"Elizabeth?" he whispered through dry, parched lips.

"Shhh . . . shhh."

Cool winds blew over him, and then the winds became birds' wings, caressing him gently, tenderly. He moaned.

Something touched his lips—a hand, a cup, both. Warmth spread through him . . . and a kind of peace, a peace he hadn't known in a long time. He drifted, letting it come.

Around midnight his fever broke. He opened his eyes, fully alert. Without sound, he turned his head slightly so he could see the room. His eyes, trained to see enemies at a great distance and under all conditions, adjusted quickly to the darkness. Elizabeth was in silhouette beside the window. A pale shaft of moonlight slipping between the folds of the closed curtain illuminated her hair.

Black Hawk studied her in silence. She was a strong woman, a brave woman. A flash of metal caught his attention. In her hands was the .44 Magnum. She was watching over him with a gun in her hands.

"Don't shoot, Elizabeth. I'm not armed."

"You're awake." She whirled toward him. He chuckled.

"That's not funny, Black Hawk."

"My friends call me Blackie; my lovers call me Hawk."

"I am neither. I'm the hostess; you're the guest." She stood up, and he saw a bit of red satin peeping from the hem of her sturdy chenille robe. So . . . Elizabeth McCade hid herself from him.

"That will soon change, Elizabeth."

"I know. As fast as you seem to bounce back, you'll be leaving in no time. Then you will be nothing to me except a bad memory."

"Do you always fight so hard against your feelings?"

"I'm not fighting; I have already conquered." She stood up and hurried toward the door. Black Hawk's voice stopped her.

"You watched over me."

She turned toward him with a certain resignation. His voice commanded her as his eyes had, Black Hawk would always command her. The knowledge was a burden she must bear. Some crazy twist of fate had set in her path the one man who could unlock the doors to her past and unleash her passions.

She gripped her gun so hard, her knuckles were white, praying all the while for strength to withstand Black Hawk's sensuous assault. Holding the neck of her robe close around her throat so not one inch of flesh would be exposed to his searching eyes, she faced him.

"You needed nourishment and medicine. I gave you both."

"You caressed my face."

"I checked your temperature. I didn't think it wise to leave you alone with such a high fever."

"I still burn, Elizabeth."

She crossed the room and leaned over his bed, pressing one hand against his brow. Her dark eyes widened as she looked at him.

"The fever has gone."

"No. I burn. . . ." He reached out and circled her throat with one hand, bracing her chin and tipping her head backward. Her breathing became harsh, and the gun slipped from her hand. It landed with a soft thump on the bed.

Black Hawk slid his other hand into the neck of her robe. She closed her eyes, moaning.

"We both burn with the same fever, Elizabeth."

The wisp of satin covering her breasts was no barrier to him. He pushed it aside. His hands were hot on her, taking liberties she allowed no man.

"You want me, Elizabeth . . . as I want you."

Every inch of her body felt sensitized. She was burning, ready to explode.

"Nooo," she moaned. His hands seduced her, bewitched her, almost drove her over the edge. With a mighty effort she conjured up the image of Mark Laton. "No."

She jerked herself upright and pulled her robe around her. Black Hawk lay against the pillows like a bronze god, waiting for the proper homage. She tore her gaze away and searched for her gun. It gleamed up from the white sheets.

"I brought my gun to use against your enemies, Black Hawk. Be warned. I won't hesitate to use it against you."

She swept from his room, clutching her robe and her big gun to her chest. The door shut with a sharp click. Black Hawk smiled into the darkness, twin passions raging through him. At the moment, the passion for battle was secondary to his passion for the woman. He would have her. He would have Elizabeth McCade.

Upstairs Elizabeth threw off her ugly robe and flung it across the back of a rocking chair. In the glow from her bedside lamp she caught her reflection in the mirror. She cupped her breasts, then ran her hands down her body, longing for the feel of other hands, *his* hands, Black Hawk's hands.

A low moaning sound escaped her lips, then suddenly she flung open her desk drawer and pulled out her diary. She needed a way to spend her passion, and for the last seven years, recording her thoughts had done that.

She wrote in bold strokes, the letters marching like soldiers across a barren landscape.

"A stranger in my house has resurrected the passion I had thought was dead. Black Hawk—he's as fierce as his name—faced me with a knife, and I faced him with a gun. And both of us knew that we were one and the same, creatures of passion destined to be together, if only to appease the gods of desire that control us. Heaven help us."

She closed her diary and went to bed, sleeping fitfully, her dreams haunted by visions of bronze hands searching her body.

"I won't lose," she said the next morning, as she pinned her hair into a French twist and donned her most severe business suit. If it weren't for her puffy lips and glazed eyes, she would look normal. She hoped she looked normal enough to fool her coworkers. Not that any of them would dare question her. She didn't encourage that kind of familiarity.

Downstairs she followed her usual routine. She ate breakfast, then read the morning paper with her coffee. Briefly she considered leaving without checking on Black Hawk, but she decided that was the cowardly thing to do, and she had never been cowardly, even when Mark Laton had brought her world crashing down around her ears and sent her back home to Mississippi.

After checking her watch to be certain she could

spare no more than five minutes in his bedroom, she carried a tray to Black Hawk. He was coming out of the bathroom, wearing his jeans.

"They say you are dead," she said, setting the tray with the morning paper on the bedside table.

"How did I die?" He lifted the coffee cup to his lips and watched her over the rim.

"You were killed with a Winchester rifle. Sheriff Wayne Blodgett found your bloodstained shirt in the woods near your ranch. The bullet was lodged in a tree, and the spent shell was in the bushes."

"Do they know who killed me?"

"No. There are many different accounts. The most interesting comes from Walter Martin and Bobby Clayburn. They say that they were out snake hunting and witnessed you being slain by a gang of long-haired hippies who stuffed your body into a sack and carried it off. Naturally they were too scared to do anything except watch."

"Walter Martin and Bobby Clayburn are on the payroll of the mall developers. They hope to demoralize my people and weaken the defense."

"Will they succeed? After all, you *are* the leader."

"There will be other leaders to take my place while I'm gone. They won't succeed."

"How can you be so sure?"

"The Chickasaws haven't lost a battle since DeSoto tried to make us slaves. Our unofficial motto is 'We are unconquered and unconquerable.'" He smiled. "We won't lose, Elizabeth."

"Should I get word to someone that you are alive?"

"No. It would be too dangerous. My people won't give up the fight, and they won't give me up for dead without convincing evidence. I'll be leaving in a few days anyhow."

Elizabeth busied herself with the tray, straightening the silverware, smoothing the napkin, rearranging the juice—anything to keep her hands and her mind occupied and off Black Hawk.

"I don't know what you like for breakfast, so I just made a little bit of everything."

"Thank you, Elizabeth."

"Don't get used to this kind of treatment, though. As soon as you're able, you can fend for yourself."

Never had a man's silence been so commanding. She lifted her gaze slowly to his and almost reeled from the impact. Black Hawk was not the kind of man who needed talk to get her attention. All he had to do was be in her presence, and everything else was forgotten. He didn't move, didn't speak, and yet she felt as if he had lassoed her heart, her mind, her body. She yearned for him, drawn by the mystique and sense of danger that surrounded him.

With an effort, she jammed her hands into her skirt pockets and clenched her fists so he wouldn't see.

"I want you to know that my sympathies are with you and your people, Black Hawk. I have always abhorred the practice of so-called "progress" without regard to the environment and to history. Progress must preserve our past as well as ensure our future. I hope you win."

He smiled. "In the basement . . . when I held my knife to your throat and felt your body against mine . . . when I smelled the fragrance of your hair and felt the passions that raged through you . . . I knew I could trust you." His smile vanished, and he moved closer to her. "You *must* not give me away, Elizabeth. I'm fighting a dangerous enemy. They wouldn't hesitate to hurt you, as they've tried to destroy me."

"Don't worry. I can take care of myself. And besides, no one would dare suspect me of harboring any man, let alone a notorious man such as you. I have a reputation—"

Suddenly she realized she had said too much. "I have to go to work," she said, whirling around to leave the room.

Black Hawk moved swiftly, catching her by the shoulders and turning her to face him. Then he tipped her face up with one hand, studying her.

"Black linen by day and red satin by night." His gaze swept over her face, searching, burning. "They are wrong, Elizabeth. You are a woman of immense fire and passion." He leaned closer to her, so close she could feel his warm breath fanning against her cheek. "You are a woman who needs to be kissed."

She thought he was going to kiss her. He looked as if he would start with her lips and work his way down to her toes. Her body tingled with anticipation, and she fought the desire that welled up inside.

His hand tightened on her face, and his eyes got so dark, she thought she was gazing into the pits of hell. Then suddenly, inexplicably, he let her go. She struggled to keep from sagging against the door frame.

"Go, Elizabeth. Go to your work and don't betray me."

She left quickly, knowing he was watching her, knowing he was staying behind in her spare bedroom, and most of all, knowing he would be there when she got back.

By hurrying she arrived at work on time. Gladys, who worked the reception desk as well as the switchboard on the first floor of Tombigbee Bluff Bank, looked at her a little funny, but she didn't comment. When Elizabeth had come back to Tombigbee Bluff seven years before, Gladys had been full of questions and good intentions.

"We thought you had gone off to Yale to study to be a teacher," she had said. "What changed your mind?"

"Nothing," Elizabeth had told her, hoping to discourage questions.

"I'll bet it was beautiful up there. Where is Yale, anyhow?"

"Connecticut."

"Oh yeah, Connecticut. I'll bet it snows up there every Christmas. . . . My friend Mavis—you remember Mavis Jarvis, don't you?—well, Mavis told me that she heard some fellow jilted you up there."

There had been no malice in her voice, only curiosity. Elizabeth had said nothing.

"That's just too bad, but it's not the end of the world. There are always more fish in the pond, as the old saying goes. Why, my boyfriend—you remember Charles Estes, don't you?—well, anyhow, he's got this friend, Jerry Morgan. Used to live up around Chicago. A real hunk . . . I could fix you up with him."

"Thank you, but no."

Gladys had made two or three more attempts to find out about her checkered past and to pull her into the mainstream of Tombigbee Bluff society, but Elizabeth had kept her secrets to herself and had refused all except the most innocent of social invitations. She went to an occasional bridal tea and bank party and church social—always places where the crowds would be large and the chances for intimacy small. There was no way she could become a total recluse. After all, she lived in a small Southern town where one of the two major pastimes was gossip. The other was backyard barbecues. Usually they went hand in hand. Reputations had been built and destroyed over a good-sized portion of pig, done to a turn.

So, when Elizabeth walked into the bank that morning, she smiled and called a cheerful greeting to Gladys and all her coworkers, then passed to her office in the loan department as if it were just another day in Tombigbee Bluff—and not the day she was lusting for a certain Chickasaw warrior hiding in her spare bedroom.

Elizabeth left work earlier than usual. Her exit raised a few eyebrows, especially Gladys's.

"I can't believe it," Gladys said. "The woman who spends most of her waking moments at the bank is leaving at a reasonable hour. Is the world coming to a end?"

"If it does, Gladys, I'm sure you'll be the first to know."

Gladys laughed as she grabbed her own purse and started for the door. "Look, Elizabeth, there's no need to be embarrassed about leaving work on time. After all, you're too young to be tied down here when you should be out partying with some handsome stud."

A vision of Black Hawk came into Elizabeth's mind. With her hand on the door, she hesitated. It was all the encouragement Gladys needed.

"Aha. You've got a boyfriend. I knew it all along. A beautiful woman like you. Who is it? Anybody we know?"

Elizabeth pulled herself together. "You're wrong, Gladys. My social life is still every bit as boring."

"Oh, shoot." Gladys looked so disappointed, Elizabeth decided to be generous and gracious, characteristics she was afraid she had neglected of late—in fact, for the last seven years.

"Cheer up, Gladys. Perhaps I'll take you up on

your invitation to meet one of the many men in your life."

"When?"

Once more she thought of Black Hawk lying in her bed with his knife slid under his pillow. "Perhaps in a couple of weeks . . . when I get up enough courage." She wasn't being honest, of course. She had never been lacking in courage. She was afraid of no man. The only thing she had lacked was the will.

Elizabeth didn't see Black Hawk when she got home. Her house was as quiet as it had always been, and seemed just as empty. For a moment she panicked.

"Oh, no. He's gone," she whispered, standing in the middle of the kitchen floor, pressing her hands over her heart.

"Your beauty makes this house come alive, Elizabeth."

She whirled toward the sound of his voice. He was leaning against her refrigerator, his knife tucked into his jeans, his naked chest lacerated with wounds.

"Don't sneak up on me like that."

"I didn't sneak. I walked quietly."

"Well, then, don't walk quietly."

"It is the Chickasaw way."

She had felt edgy all day. Seeing him, she felt testy as well. Her life had been safe and sensible until he drifted into her cellar, and now nothing made any sense.

Her high heels tapped out an angry rhythm as she marched toward the refrigerator door and flung it open. His expression never changed: He looked as aloof as the finest bronze statue on a museum shelf.

"While you're in my house, you'll do things my way," she said.

Black Hawk said nothing. *Don't do this to me*, she wanted to yell, though he was doing nothing except standing there.

Slowly she turned her head to look at him. That was her first mistake.

"You aren't handling this well, Elizabeth."

She slammed the refrigerator shut. "Dammit, Hawk." She grabbed his shoulders. Touching him was her second mistake. The heat started in her hands and worked its way through the rest of her. She wet her lips, trying to put out the fire.

"You called me Hawk." His eyes were very dark.

"It was a slip of the tongue."

She started to pull her hands away, but he held her fast, hauling her so close, she could feel the full length of him.

"Only my lovers call me Hawk." His hands moved into her hair, loosening the pins and casting them onto the kitchen floor. The heavy mass fell down around her shoulders, and he tangled his hands in it.

Her breathing came in short bursts. Neither of them spoke. It was almost as if they had given up their wills and fate had taken over. Hawk's eyes were predatory as he lowered his head toward hers.

She knew what was going to happen next, knew it and wanted to run, knew it and wanted to scream. But she did neither, for more than anything, she wanted to be kissed. Not by just any man—but by Hawk, the man who held her in his spell.

"Hawk," she whispered.

"You want me."

"No."

"I want you."

His arms tightened as he backed her against the

kitchen counter. She could feel the size and heat of him. Her head began to spin.

"Someone could come."

"The blinds are closed, and I saw you lock the door."

He slid her jacket off, and she heard it land on the kitchen floor. Bending low, he pressed his lips against her throat.

"Such soft skin, Elizabeth. Made for a man's touch." His tongue sent shivers skittering along her skin. Unconsciously she reached for him, splaying her fingers along the back of his neck and pressing his head closer.

"Oh . . . please . . . nooo."

"Your lips say no, but your body says yes."

His mouth slammed down on hers, and she was lost, caught in the primitive passion that overtook her.

Three

Hawk had meant merely to sample her lips, but the instant he touched her, he knew he had to have more. What was there about this woman that drove him mad? He wanted her as he had wanted no other woman.

Without regard to his injuries or his responsibilities or his situation, he took his time with her, sliding his mouth over hers until he felt her response. It wasn't long in coming, and he was amazed at the intensity. He had been right: Elizabeth McCade was a woman of fire.

He lifted her onto the cabinet and slid his hand under her skirt, his mouth never leaving hers. Her outward garments were a modern-day suit of armor, but underneath she was dressed to please. He felt warm flesh at the top of her stockings, and tiny French-cut panties under her garter belt. She was a rich treasure waiting to be discovered. He explored without restraint.

His mouth left hers and roamed down the side of her throat. She leaned her head back to give him access.

"Hawk," she whispered, over and over.

He knew then—knew she was willing, knew she was ready, knew he could have her. He slid his knife out of his belt so it wouldn't bite into her tender skin, then pressed closer so he was fitted perfectly between her knees.

"You will be mine, Elizabeth," he said, his hands skimming her shoulders and sliding underneath her blouse. "All mine." The silk whispered as he undid her buttons.

She was swaying on the cabinet, making a soft murmuring sound, like night wind singing through the forest. He felt primitive and powerful with her, invincible.

He pushed aside her silk blouse and the wisp of lace covering her breasts. Her skin was warm and satiny.

"You are beautifully created, Elizabeth, a supreme work of the gods." He caressed her with gentleness and wonder, as if she were precious and breakable. He hadn't expected to feel this way. Once she had shown her willingness, he had thought to take her on the kitchen counter, swiftly and without feeling. Appeasing his appetite had been uppermost in his mind. Now something else was on his mind—admiring, wondering, *feeling* the specialness of the woman in his arms. And he knew, as surely as he knew the ways of the moon and the stars, that once he took this woman, she would forever be a part of him.

And yet, he wanted her still. He lowered his head and pressed his face into her scented flesh. He inhaled deeply, then began a slow, deliberate seduction with his lips and tongue.

Elizabeth was with him all the way, the heat spreading, building until Hawk felt as if he held the burning sun in his arms. He slid his hand along her legs, caressing, searching, until at last he found what he sought.

"Nooo." She spasmed, once, twice, then stiffened. "Stop. Oh, please, stop." She pushed against his shoulders.

"Elizabeth?" He lifted his head and looked at her. Her face was flushed with desire, but her eyes were wild with unnamed fears.

"Hawk." She grabbed his shoulders, swaying a moment. Then a new determination came into her face, and she dug her fingers into his flesh. "We must not do this."

"Why not, Elizabeth?" His own breathing was ragged, and his heart was pumping so hard, he felt as if he had run cross-country.

Elizabeth fumbled with her clothing. He reached out and helped her.

"Why not?" he asked once more, gentler this time.

"Because . . ." She bent over her buttons, and her hair swung down and obscured her face.

Still pressed against her, he waited. He could feel the trembling in her body.

"Are you afraid of me, Elizabeth?" She said nothing, and he reached out and touched her cheek. "There is no need to be afraid. I would never hurt you."

"It's not that." She lifted her face, and he saw that it was drained of color. "I'm not afraid of you; I'm afraid of myself."

Hawk sought to understand. "I'm not asking for commitment, Elizabeth—merely appeasement. I judged your appetites to be as big as my own."

"This has to do with more than sexual appetites."

She made a move, and he lifted her off the counter. He didn't release her immediately, but gripped her shoulders and scrutinized her face.

"Tell me," he commanded.

"No. I can't. It's private."

Never before had Hawk felt the need to know a woman's intimate thoughts. But now he was consumed with the need to know the secrets of Elizabeth McCade.

"What are your secrets, Elizabeth? What demons haunt you?"

She jerked free of him and bent over to pick up her jacket. Her expression was guarded as she slid her arms into the jacket and buttoned it securely at her waist. Her hands trembled as she swept her hair off her neck in an attempt to restore it to its prim knot. But she had no hairpins. They were scattered on the floor.

Hawk picked them up, one by one. Silently he handed them to her.

Equally silent, she took the pins and jammed them into her hair. Her color returned, and her trembling ceased.

"I will not be touched again," she said.

"I will not touch you again . . . until you ask me to."

"I'll never ask."

He smiled at her and retrieved his knife from the kitchen counter. Tucking it into his belt, he faced her.

"We are alike, Elizabeth. You will ask." He left her quickly, never looking back.

He heard her leave the kitchen, heard her footsteps on the stairs, heard her bedroom door slam. His flesh wounds ached and smarted, but not nearly as much as the wound to his spirit. It wasn't a sense of rejection that pained him; it was a sense that he had somehow failed Elizabeth, that he had been the source of great anxiety to her.

Black Hawk stood in the hallway, pondering her behavior and his own. What were her secrets to him? There was no answer to his question, only the overwhelming feeling that he had to know.

• • • •

Upstairs in her bedroom, Elizabeth sat at her desk staring at her diary, which lay open to an entry dated more than seven years before.

"It is a forbidden love we have embarked upon," she had written in a round, schoolgirl scrawl. "Dr. Laton—Mark—is a professor and I am a student. Long-standing tradition and school policy both state that we should not be together."

Elizabeth propped her head on her hands and stared into space. They had been together—many times. Mark had pursued her until she gave in. He had been her teacher, her mentor, her idol. He had been older and wiser, and she had been young and naive.

She glanced down at the diary once more and continued to read. "Mark took me to the Celestial Hideaway two counties away. We sat at a table in the corner and gazed at each other across the red-checkered cloth. 'I want to make love to you, Elizabeth,' he said in that deep voice of his. 'I want to teach you the ways of a man and a woman.' My protests were weak and he knew it. That very night I allowed him to carry me back to his office in the English building. He undressed me and laid me on the small cot. I was scared at first, but he was kind and patient and proved himself as good a teacher of love as he is of Chaucer."

Elizabeth skipped a few entries, then read, "I dream of nothing but Mark, of the day we can be together in public places, of the day I will wear his ring and claim him as mine. He laughs when I tell him my dreams, then hushes me with a kiss. That's all it takes—one kiss, one touch, and I am his geisha. That's what he calls me. He has taught me well, so well that I sit in my other classes, dreaming of new ways I can please him. He says I am made for love, and I can't deny it. It's all I can think about."

Elizabeth flung the diary across the room.

"Damn you, Mark Laton."

"Elizabeth?" Hawk tapped at her door. "Are you all right?"

"Go away. I don't want to see you."

The door opened, and he walked in with a tray loaded with food and brightened by red-checkered napkins and a lighted candle. Elizabeth froze.

"Where did you get that?"

"I made it myself—with much effort and will-power. No sacrifice is too great for the woman who has given me refuge."

"Not the food . . . the napkins."

"I found them in the linen closet."

She knew she was overreacting, but she couldn't seem to help herself. Red-checkered anything, especially when combined with candlelight, always reminded her of Mark.

Hawk was watching her carefully, as if she might explode at any minute, and he wanted to know which direction to jump in order to pick up the pieces. Well, she wouldn't give him that satisfaction. She pulled herself together and marched toward him.

"Thank you for preparing my dinner. That was thoughtful of you."

"I made enough for two."

She didn't want to see him. She didn't want to sit at a table with him. She didn't even want to be in the same room as him. But she wasn't about to admit it. Surely she could handle sharing one meal.

She took the tray and glanced around her room. The bedside table would do; she could pull up two chairs. But she wasn't about to be trapped with Hawk in her bedroom for the next thirty minutes.

"We'll eat downstairs."

They made their way downstairs side by side, saying nothing. When they reached her dining room, she blew out the candle and tucked the red-checkered napkins into a drawer of her antique sideboard, replacing them with white linen. Hawk noticed, but she didn't care. She was not going to offer any explanations or any apologies.

He pulled out her chair, and she thanked him. All very polite and proper. It amused her to think that they were the same two people who had almost made love on the kitchen counter only an hour earlier.

She expected the meal to be a strained affair, but Hawk surprised her. He was at ease and full of great charm, speaking on a variety of subjects that caught her interest—literature, entertainment, and especially politics as it affected the world they lived in.

They agreed on much and argued about little. It seemed their only bone of contention was the unspoken one—passion and how to handle it.

"You have a chess set," he said near the end of their meal.

"Yes." She smiled. "Given your habit of snooping, I suppose you can tell me everything I have in this house."

"It's called scouting, not snooping."

She liked his sense of humor. In fact, there were a lot of things she was learning to like about Black Hawk—aside from the obvious. It still made her insides shake just to look at him.

"Shall we play a game?"

"What?" she asked, temporarily distracted by her thoughts.

"Chess, Elizabeth."

He had a big, free laugh. Suddenly she was furious at Mark Laton, furious that he had taken away her ability to be totally relaxed with men such as Black Hawk. She was so tired of constantly being on guard.

"Certainly. I'll play a game with you." She got up from the table. "I trust you'll be a worthy opponent."

"I am lethal."

She already knew how lethal he could be. Together they stacked the dishes, then went into her den. It was cozy, with comfortable stuffed chairs, colorful rugs, and lots of lamps.

"Do you always keep your curtains drawn, Elizabeth?" Hawk asked as he set up the board on the game table.

"Why do you ask?"

"If anyone should come unexpectedly, would they notice anything different about your house?"

"No. I like privacy. And don't worry. No one will come."

They set up their pieces and started the game. Both played with great skill, but Hawk quickly won the first game.

"You're an aggressive player," Elizabeth said. "Do you always go on the attack?"

"Always. I am a warrior."

"In real life as well as in games, if all the stories I read about you are correct."

"They are correct in that assessment. Although a few of my exploits have been exaggerated."

The story of your holding the mayor's roast pig hostage while a hundred and fifty guests starved?"

"True." He laughed.

"I don't remember what that was all about."

"He refused to consider or even discuss a proposal that would require recycling. I think we should be caretakers of the world we live in and not destroyers of it."

"And what about the tale of your riding into the

boardroom of the city planning commission on your horse?"

"It was the only way I could get their attention. That was over a small zoning problem."

"It wasn't so small, as I recall. You were trying to keep one of our city's few remaining tracts of wooded land from being turned into an industrial park."

"The industrial parks we have are not filled. If the planning commission had gotten its way, there would soon be no place left for the people of Tombigbee Bluff."

They set up the board and started another game as they talked. Hawk checkmated her in an amazingly short time.

"Don't expect to always win so easily."

"But I do." He smiled. "I don't think you're paying attention."

It was true. Only half her mind was on the game; the other half was on her opponent. She vowed to herself to do better.

They both played with savage intensity. When she threatened his king, conversation ceased.

The room was perfectly still except for the occasional click of marble chess pieces against the board. Outside, a summer rain began to fall, tapping lightly against the windowpanes and the old tin roof of Elizabeth's ancestral home. Gentle breezes stirred the pine trees to a melodic whispering.

Black Hawk looked up from the chessboard. "It's cozy in here, Elizabeth . . . just the two of us."

She didn't comment, but she had felt the coziness as well. After seven years of living as a virtual recluse, it felt good to have a guest in her house, to share a simple game of chess.

They gazed at each other over the chessboard for a long time, and then, almost self-consciously, they both turned their attention back to the game. Both reached out at the same time, and their hands collided over one of her pawns.

They looked at each other once more. Never had a man's eyes reflected as much emotion as Hawk's. All of Elizabeth's breath seemed to leave her body.

"Pardon me," she whispered.

"I believe it was my turn," he said.

"Certainly." She would not dare admit that she had forgotten. He had accused her once of not having her mind on the game. She wouldn't give him another chance.

She forced her attention back to her chess pieces, and played out the game to its conclusion. The rain had picked up speed and was whipping the house in a fury by the time Elizabeth and Hawk had made all their moves.

"I believe this is stalemate," he said.

"So it is. Nobody won."

"You're right. Neither of us won." His eyes seemed to burn through her. "Another game?"

"No. It's very late."

She straightened the chess pieces and left the board set for a new game, while he sat in the chair, watching her. Her gaze slid sideways. His naked chest was still crisscrossed with marks, but they were no longer red and angry.

He was healing rapidly. Soon he would be gone.

"You are responsible, Elizabeth."

"For what?"

"My rapid healing."

"Do you read minds?"

"No. I read faces. You were watching me, studying my wounds."

She didn't bother to deny it.

"You have skilled hands, Elizabeth," he added.

The double meaning in his words was intentional, she was sure. It was on the tip of her tongue to say that she should have skilled hands: Mark had taught her well. Instead, she started for the door.

"Good night, Black Hawk," she said, careful to use both his names.

"Sweet dreams, Elizabeth."

Upstairs in her bedroom, she knew her dreams wouldn't be sweet. They never were. They would be tortured and painful, full of visions from the past.

She undressed and drew her bath, taking her time. She was in no hurry to go to bed. The bed hadn't been a sanctuary for her for the last seven years.

Dressed in a gown of vivid blue, she stood at the window, looking out at the rain, paralyzed by memories almost too painful to bear. Downstairs Hawk would be climbing into bed. Perhaps he was already there, stretched out naked on the sheets.

All the feelings he had unleashed in her came roaring to the surface, a raging river sweeping away everything in its path. Almost, she could feel Hawk's hands on her. Almost, she could feel his lips on hers. She wanted to go to him; she wanted to be with him. It had been so long, so *long* since she had needed a man—and not just any man. Hawk. Only Hawk.

She turned from the window and actually started across the room, when she heard Mark Laton's parting words echoing from her past.

"Your first mistake was in trusting me. Your second was in falling in love. I didn't hurt you, Elizabeth. You hurt yourself."

She stood very still, torn by indecision and doubts. She had been running for seven years, hiding herself away in her shuttered house, defining her life by working hours at the bank and the few pitiful social exchanges she allowed. Safe. Her life was safe.

And she was stifling herself to death.

"Damn you," she said, clenching her fists and facing the Mark Laton who lurked in her subconscious mind. "You ruined my life once. You destroyed my virginity, my dreams, my profession, my future. I won't let you destroy my present. I won't!"

Her silk gown whispered as she walked toward her door. She was going to Hawk. He had said the next move was up to her, and she was making it.

But this time she was older, smarter, and much, much wiser. She was not going downstairs expecting love and marriage, a cottage for two, and happily ever after. She was merely seeking companionship and release. Two days, three, and then it would be over. Nobody would be hurt. Hawk would leave, and she'd go back to her safe life.

She hurried, excitement pulsing through her. When she reached his door, she didn't hesitate, but pushed it open and walked boldly inside.

The rain still whipped at the windows, and not even a sliver of moonlight relieved the intense blackness. She strained her eyes, searching for Hawk among the shadows.

"You came." His voice was strong and beautiful. If he had been aroused from sleep, she couldn't tell it.

"Yes." Now that she was in his room, she hesitated, not sure how to proceed.

"I knew you would."

"Did you?"

"Yes. I have already claimed you. You are mine, Elizabeth."

Atuned now to the darkness, she saw him get off the bed. He was tall and noble and magnificent as he walked slowly toward her. She trembled, and her resolve almost shattered.

"There is nothing to fear, Elizabeth." He was

standing before her now, not touching, merely watching her.

"I'm not afraid," she whispered.

"Come." He took her hand and led her to the bed. "I am Hawk. Together we will soar."

Four

Hawk had known Elizabeth would come to him. Stretched on top of his bed still dressed in jeans and moccasins, he had waited for her. Now he released her and snapped on the small lamp.

"Why?" she asked, nodding toward the light.

"I want to see you." Slowly he circled her, taking her in from all angles. Her gown was slashed to the waist, front and back, and slit high on both sides. She had a beautifully defined body, tight musculature, satiny skin. He looked forward to possessing her.

"Walk for me, Elizabeth," he commanded softly.

She moved with the grace of a woman aware of her own sexuality and comfortable with it. The satin gown revealed long, enticing glimpses of leg. Her hair was down, rippling like a bolt of black silk in the lamplight.

When she reached the door, she placed her hand on the handle as if she intended to leave, then glanced at him over her shoulder with a sensuous pout.

"You won't leave until you get what you want," he said.

She turned slowly. "No. I won't go until I have you, Hawk," she whispered. "Every inch of you."

His eyes became hooded and his breath raspy as she ran her hands seductively down the length of her body. Elizabeth McCade was the sexiest woman he had ever known. Even with her clothes on, on the other side of the room, she managed to make him feel as if he were already inside her.

"Do you like your loving slow and leisurely, or fast and furious?" she asked.

"Both ways . . . and then some."

She wet her lips with her tongue as she arched one shoulder. Her gown strap slid down as far as her elbow. With her gaze smoky and promising, she reached across and pushed the strap over her wrist until she had bared her right breast.

"For you," she said.

He started toward her. She lifted her long hair off her neck and let it filter through her fingers until it curtained her breast.

Hawk bent down and blew the hair out of his way. Then he touched his tongue to her nipple, lightly, teasingly. She moaned. He wrapped one arm around her waist, flattened one palm over her heart, and suckled her until her heart was racing.

When he lifted his head, she smiled at him. "You have a magic mouth, Hawk."

"You inspire the magic, my beauty."

He peeled her gown away until it lay in a dark blue pool at their feet. He explored her then, taking his time, using his hands and his mouth to touch each sensitive area of her body.

"You are honey, Elizabeth; I am the bear who feeds on you." He cupped her hips and pulled her closer. He felt the enormous passion in her, the intensity, the fire. She flamed at his touch, burning so hot, he felt as if he were melting, melting until he was a part of her.

Her fingernails dug into his shoulders, but he didn't feel any pain. He felt only joy, as if he were soaring across the sky like his namesake, tasting every wonderful freedom the world had to offer.

At last, when her knees threatened to buckle, Hawk lifted her and carried her to the bed. With her dark hair spread against the white sheets, she looked exotic, almost Indian.

He put his hand on his belt, but she reached up and stopped him. "I want to undress you."

"Yes," he said.

She sat up and pressed her face against his stomach. Her warm breath fanned his skin, and her tongue sent shivers through him.

"You still wear your knife." She pulled his weapon from his belt. The blade glinted in the lamplight.

"A warrior is always prepared."

She ran her fingers over his blue-jean-clad thighs. "I can see that."

He caught her chin and tipped her face upward. "My blade is swift and mighty and true, Elizabeth."

Slowly she smiled. "Show me."

There was a whispering sound as she slid his jeans off. Hawk poised above her, drawing out the anticipation until the room was fairly humming with tension. Elizabeth raked one fingernail lightly down his chest and across his abdomen, lower and lower until her hands were curled around him.

"Show me, Hawk. Now."

He came to her in one smooth motion. Their joining was so exquisite, so perfect, that both of them cried out in wonder.

"I knew, Elizabeth . . . from the moment I saw you, I knew we would be like this together."

"Hawk." She tightened her arms around him, and he began an ancient rhythm. At first he was a gentle brook, meandering slowly through warm meadows damp with dew. Quickly he became a raging river, cutting a mighty path through the earth, digging so deeply, he reached the earth's hot center. The tumult roared in his ears, and he called out his victory cry in Muskhogean, the language of his people.

He held her close for a while, murmuring ancient love words in her ears. She was so still, he thought she had fallen asleep; then she lifted herself on one elbow and looked down at him, smiling.

"Do you think the battle is over, my mighty warrior?"

He cupped one cheek, tangling his fingers in her damp hair. "Do you dare challenge me?"

"Yes."

He laughed, delighted with her. She was all he had imagined and more—much, much more. Elizabeth McCade was a woman with appetites to equal his own. The fates had been smiling on him the day he'd fallen into her cellar.

Her eyes grew bright with desire, and she bent over him. Her silky hair whispered against his skin. As her hands and mouth moved over him, Elizabeth began to speak softly. It was a while before he realized she was quoting erotic love sonnets. By then he didn't care what she was saying, as long as she kept doing what she was doing.

"You are a sorceress, Elizabeth," he said, groaning as she worked her magic. He made a move to rise over her and take her once more.

"Not yet." She pressed him lightly on the chest, and he lay back against the sheets, every fiber of his being straining toward her, aching to be a part of her.

Suddenly she stopped. He moaned her name.

"Do you want me?" she asked, looking down at him.

"More than the parched earth wants the rain, more than the panting buck seeks the doe, more than a dying man longs for life."

"That will do for starters," she said, smiling sweetly. And then Elizabeth McCade took charge. She carried him on a wild roller coaster ride that lasted far into the night.

Just before dawn pinked the sky, she gathered her silk gown off the floor and stole across the room. Hawk lay against the sheets, watching her go. When she reached the door, he spoke.

"You are mine, Elizabeth."

"No, Hawk," she said, turning slowly. "You are *mine*."

The door closed softly behind her. Hawk closed his eyes, his appetite fully sated.

Outside in the hallway, Elizabeth leaned against the door, her heart hammering. Her lips felt bruised and puffy, and her body tingled. No passion burns hotter than one so long denied, she thought.

She bit her lip to keep from groaning aloud, for she didn't want Hawk to hear. As far as he was concerned, she was a woman taking advantage of the situation for a brief liaison. And that's what she had started out to do. When she had come down the stairs, she'd had every intention of using Hawk to satisfy her needs.

What had happened? At what point had her actions become more than need? When he'd first touched her? When he'd entered her? After his seed had filled her body?

She pressed her face to her hands, doubling over in the hallway. Hawk was no longer a need she could satisfy, someone she could make love to and walk away from: He was an obsession.

Elizabeth's stomach lurched as memories came back to her. She must not repeat the mistakes of her past. Hawk was no Mark Laton. There was a nobility, a strength of character, a goodness about him that Mark had never possessed. No, it wasn't Hawk she was afraid of, it was herself. With Mark she had lost all control, had let her passions rule her life. She must not do the same thing with Hawk. She *would* not. Balling her hands into fists, she repeated the vow to herself. *I will not let passion rule this time. I will take what I want, then walk away. I will be in charge.*

Elizabeth turned and ran her hands lightly across the bedroom door. "Sleep well, my noble warrior," she whispered, then walked away.

She didn't see him the next morning before she left for work. Considering how they had spent the night, she supposed he was sleeping.

Elizabeth was too energized to sleep. She walked with a new spring to her step, moved with a new confidence. When she entered her workplace, she felt as if she could accomplish miracles. She caught herself humming aloud as she sat at her desk going over her morning reports.

"My goodness," she said to herself, laughing. Then she swiveled her chair and looked out the window. She saw Hawk everywhere, in the solid oak tree that graced the corner of the bank parking lot, in the hot sun pouring through the window, in the bird that suddenly rose from the branches and soared toward the sky. It was only a blackbird, but still she thought of Hawk.

She spent the day dreaming about him, with her eyes wide open. She imagined what he would say to her when she got home from work. She imagined what he would do, where he would take her, where he would touch her. It was all she could do to stay in the bank until closing time. Twice she thought of pleading sickness and going home, just to be with Hawk.

"Elizabeth McCade," she whispered to herself when the day was finally over and she was roaring down the highway toward home, "you are a wild woman." Then she threw back her head and laughed. It felt good to be wild and free again.

Hawk met her at the front door.

"I've waited for you all day," he said, pinning her against the wall, exploring her with his lips and his hands.

She dropped her purse and her car keys onto the wooden floor as she wrapped her arms around him. She didn't care where they landed: She was once more in the arms of Hawk.

His mouth was hot and demanding on hers. Their passion escalated quickly, exploding in a frenzy of motion. He pushed her skirt high around her hips and braced her against the wall. Then he took her with a fury that left them both panting.

"I've wanted this all day, Hawk," she said, leaning her head against his chest."

"So have I, Elizabeth."

He carried her upstairs, placed her on the bed, and tenderly undressed her. She lay quietly while he went into the bathroom. She heard the taps turning, heard water running, heard the rattle of bottles as he found bubble bath and dumped it in the tub.

She stretched, feeling languorous and decadent. When he came back into the room, she smiled at him.

"There's nothing like having a love slave in the house," she said.

He stalked her, his eyes bright with laughter. When he was standing over the bed, he slowly stripped off his jeans. "Who is the slave, Elizabeth? You or me?"

"Both of us," she whispered, reaching for him, reminded of the words they had spoken on the cellar stairs the first day he had come into her life.

He carried her into the bathroom, and together they got into the tub, heedless of the tight squeeze. They frolicked in the bubble bath, laughing and teasing each other. Their play quickly changed to passion, and they came together in the water.

Afterward, he wrapped her in a towel and carried her to the bed again. She traced the scars on his wet chest.

"You'll be leaving soon."

"Yes. We don't have much time left together."

"How long?"

"Until tomorrow." She sucked in her breath. He cupped her face, circling his thumbs on her chin. "I leave tomorrow, Elizabeth."

Neither of them said anything. They didn't have to: Their body language said it all. Whatever emotions they felt were so tightly controlled, their bodies were rigid with the effort. Suddenly they both exploded.

"Hawk." She cried his name as she reached for him.

He pinned her to the bed, holding her arms high above her head.

"Say you want me, Elizabeth."

"Yes, Hawk. Oh, yes."

The evening shadows lengthened and the moon started its course across the night sky. Hawk and Elizabeth never noticed. Stars came out, one by one, reflecting their brightness against the windowpanes, but the two on the bed paid them no heed.

Around midnight a visitor came calling. He padded lightly through the kitchen and sneaked quietly up the stairs. He hesitated on the landing a moment, getting his bearings, then he eased through the half-open door of Elizabeth's bedroom.

Hawk clamped his hand over Elizabeth's mouth at the same time he reached for his knife. He searched the darkness, looking for a shadow, a glimpse of light clothing, anything that would give him a clue about the intruder. There was nothing . . . only the soft scurrying sound that had alerted him, and the instinctive sense that he and Elizabeth were not alone.

He decided to take an aggressive posture. Still holding his hand securely over Elizabeth's mouth, he spoke.

"I have a knife, and it's aimed at your heart. Make one move, and you are dead." With the blade poised to throw, he released Elizabeth and snapped on the bedside lamp.

A big tomcat marched across the floor and took his position in a cat basket beside the window.

"Why didn't you tell me you had a cat, Elizabeth?"

"I don't. He's a stray who sometimes comes to visit."

"How does he get in? Through that old cat door in the kitchen?"

"Yes."

"You have a soft heart for strays, don't you?" He smiled.

"Only cats, dogs, birds. Especially birds." She ran her hands through his hair.

"What kind?"

"Hawks."

He kissed her lightly, then stood up and pulled on his jeans.

"What are you doing?" she asked.

"I'm going to check things out."

She didn't have to ask why. A cat had sneaked up on him. He was wondering what else might have sneaked in under the cover of darkness.

"Be careful, Hawk."

"Wait right here, Elizabeth. I'll be back." He snapped off the lamp and disappeared.

He moved as quickly and quietly as a phantom. Elizabeth hugged her arms around herself. Tomorrow he would leave just that quickly. There would be no sign that he had ever been there. No sign except the one inside her. Hawk was indelibly stamped on her heart. She wondered how she would survive the days after he had gone. But she would. He had given her great pleasure; the best way to repay him was to let him go without fanfare. He had made it perfectly clear that their relationship was based on one thing—appeasing their appetites.

Apparently, he couldn't handle more than a brief affair, and neither could she. She wished they could have a few more days together, but as it was, she was dangerously close to falling in love with him. And that would be disastrous. Her memories of falling in love were all too painful.

She hugged herself tighter and waited, waited for her Hawk to come out of the darkness once more so that together they could soar to those places where loneliness and fear did not exist.

Hawk stayed in the black night longer than necessary. There were no intruders in Elizabeth's house or on her property. Of that he was absolutely certain. Still, he hesitated to go back to her— which was ridiculous, of course. He had known from the beginning that he would leave her, known that she didn't belong to him, that she could never belong to him.

He was a warrior. Although he no longer rode

into battle armed with bow and arrow as his ancestors had, he was still fighting the same enemy: He was battling those who would destroy his home and eventually his people. The battles were much more sophisticated and the enemy much more subtle. But politics was a dirty and sometimes deadly game, and those who fought against the power and money mongers set themselves in a dangerous position. There was no way he would subject a woman to the kind of life he led, always on the edge of danger, always the point-man, always the target.

As he circled the grounds once more, he thought of his enemy. The fight over his ancestral land would soon be over. He and his people would be victorious. But there would be other battles, other enemies. Modern man was selfish and greedy. In his hell-bent desire to gain money and power, man was slowly and systematically destroying the world he lived in, with absolutely no thought to future generations—to the air they would breathe, the water they would drink, the kind of world they would inherit.

Hawk's ancestors for generations before him had fought for a better, cleaner world, a world in which man lived in harmony with nature; and so would he continue to fight. Hawk would remain strong, and he would fight alone.

Even as he made that vow, his appetite for Elizabeth grew almost to the boiling point. He would have to leave her the following day, or else he might never want to leave her at all.

"Elizabeth McCade, you have bewitched me," he said aloud as he hurried back to her bed.

She called in sick to the bank the next morning. "Gladys," she said into the downstairs telephone, "will you connect me with Quentin in loans?"

"What in the world's the matter, Elizabeth? Why aren't you at work this morning?"

"I'm afraid I've come down with something."

"Oh. Too bad. I'll connect you."

Hawk smiled at her over an enormous omelet. After she had hung up and joined him, he took her hand and ran it over his bare chest.

"What have you come down with, Elizabeth?"

"Lust."

"It must be catching."

"Are all Indians smug," she said, laughing, "or is it just you?"

"All Chickasaws. We are a superior breed."

"Don't say that word."

"Chickasaw?" he teased.

"The other one."

Hawk slowly pushed his plate away and stood up. "Could you be more specific, Elizabeth?" he said, reaching for her.

She wrapped her arms around him and nuzzled his chest. "Breed," she whispered.

"Ahh, yes." He pushed open her robe and began to caress her breasts. "Is this what you had in mind?"

"More."

"This?" His hands moved over her. "This . . . and this." He stripped her of her robe and lifted her onto the kitchen table. In one powerful move he was inside her, and both of them were lost. For a while they would hold time at bay. He knew he should go, and she knew he wouldn't stay; but for the time being they denied the truth with their loving.

Hawk stayed with her until sunset. They were in the guest bedroom downstairs, with Elizabeth stretched across the covers in beautiful disarray, and Hawk standing over her, tucking his knife into his belt.

"You're leaving," she said.

"Yes."

They stared at each other. Both of them wanted to speak, but there didn't seem to be much to say. They had already said good-bye. They had spent the day telling each other good-bye in a thousand inventive ways. Both of them were exhausted, physically and emotionally.

"Don't forget your rifle," she finally said, breaking the long silence.

"I won't."

Still he didn't move, but stood over the bed, watching her with eyes as black as the pits of hell. A quietness came over them again, and Elizabeth blinked her eyes to fight back tears.

Hawk put one hand tenderly on her cheek. "Elizabeth . . ."

"Go," she said, looking up at him. "Go quickly."

"It is best." He started toward the door.

She watched until his hand was on the doorknob, and then she couldn't bear it any longer. "Hawk!" He turned around. He was so still, he might have been cast in bronze. "Good luck," she whispered.

"Thank you, Elizabeth," he said, and then he was gone.

She collapsed against the wrinkled sheets, too spent to move, too exhausted to cry. It was over. Hawk was now a part of her past.

Hawk collected his rifle in the kitchen pantry. When he saw Elizabeth's nickel-plated .44 Magnum with the eight-inch barrel, he almost went back to her. But he knew that would be a mistake.

His interlude with Elizabeth was over. He couldn't afford to go back now; he had to go forward—into battle. Nothing, not even a woman with hair as dark as night and eyes that held his soul could make him turn from his purpose.

As he passed from her cellar into the secret passageway that had brought him to her, he briefly gazed back. "Good-bye, Elizabeth McCade," he said, then plunged into the ruined tunnel that would lead him home.

Elizabeth learned of Black Hawk's exploits through the newspapers and the reports on the local television station. "Black Hawk Lives," the headlines proclaimed the day after he had left her. There was even a picture of him, magnificent as he sat on his black stallion, granting his interview to the press. "We will never back down," he was quoted as saying. "We will fight to the end for what we believe to be right. We fight not merely for ourselves, but for all people. We fight to preserve the past and ensure the future."

She saw the interview on the six o'clock news and again at ten. Black Hawk dominated her den, almost as if he had stepped off the television screen and come back to her. Sitting on her sofa, Elizabeth clenched her hands into fists and bit down hard on her lip. She wished he had come back. She wished he had given up his battle and moved in with her so that she could keep him forever, a love prisoner in her bedroom.

"Elizabeth McCade," she said aloud, "you are a selfish, depraved woman."

Having given herself that small pep talk, she got off the couch and paced the floor. Why as it that losing Black Hawk hurt more than losing Mark

Laton? She didn't even want to think about it. She had to put it out of her mind.

She clicked the television off and went upstairs to write in her diary. But writing was no longer a release. There was only one thing that would provide that, only one man. Hawk. And he was no longer hers.

Dressed in the blue gown that Hawk had stripped from her body, she climbed into bed and hugged her arms around herself. She thought she might die from loneliness.

Five

The summer days dragged by. Elizabeth counted the hours since Hawk had gone, then she counted the days, and finally the weeks.

She could no longer stand her life. It was dull and lonely. The things she had once considered safe—going directly home after work, shunning all but an absolute minimum of social engagements, shutting herself away from the world—began to pall.

She was restless, filled with a strange new energy that seemed to be flowing directly from her heart. She searched the papers, looking for something to do, someplace to go—a movie, a concert, anything to get her out of the house. Suddenly she froze. There was going to be a rally on the town square that very evening, a gathering of citizens concerned about "progress without conscience." Black Hawk would be the speaker.

Elizabeth's hands shook as she laid the paper aside. What she was going to do was foolish, even dangerous. She was going to the rally—not out of civic duty, not out of social conscience. No, she was not driven by pure motives at all. She was going to see Hawk.

Hawk saw Elizabeth on the fringes of the crowd. He was standing on the makeshift stage, urging support of his cause in passionate prose when he saw her. She was wearing a stern suit, and her hair was tightly bound by pins, but he had never wanted a woman as much as he wanted her. His voice never faltered. He stood on the stage as if nothing had happened, continuing his speech, but his heart and soul and spirit had flown across the space that separated them. In his mind he had her in his arms; he was pulling the pins from her hair, stripping off her severe suit to reveal the sexy, lacy lingerie he knew she would be wearing underneath.

He finished the speech to thunderous applause, then climbed down from the stage and started toward her. The crowd hampered him. He was stopped for questions, for congratulations, for interviews. Out of the corner of his eye he saw that she lingered, waiting for him.

He had known she would.

Finally he was able to reach her side. She stood in the shadows of the World War II monument in a corner of the square.

"You came to see me, Elizabeth."

"Yes."

"You came to join my cause?"

"I've always been sympathetic to your cause. I needed no persuading. Though you do have great powers of persuasion."

They studied each other in the darkness. Around them, the crowd began to dissipate. Soon they would be entirely alone.

"I don't want you to be seen alone with me, Elizabeth. My enemies are dangerous."

He reached out and touched her cheek so swiftly, so briefly, she didn't even see him move. After his hand was gone, she had only the warm spot on her skin to tell her that he'd touched her there.

"It's not your cause that draws me, Hawk. It's you."

"Elizabeth . . . We must not continue."

"I know." She fought against the urge to touch his lips. "I just had to see you again, Hawk, in the flesh. I had to convince myself that you are real." She bit down hard on her lower lip. "Our time together seems like a dream."

"No, my beauty. It was real."

His gaze burned over her once more, and then he was gone. Elizabeth sagged against the monument. All she had done was see the man, speak briefly to him. And yet she felt as if she had just spent an hour in his arms.

She had come looking for trouble, and she had found it. One look at Hawk, and she was totally out of control. At that moment she would do anything, go anywhere, risk everything to be in his arms once more.

Fortunately for her, he had had the good sense to walk away. She was safe. As she left the town square she wondered why being safe didn't feel good anymore.

When she got home she stripped off all her clothes, ripped the pins from her hair, and scrubbed herself under the shower until she felt raw, as if she could wash Hawk out of her system. She dressed in the skimpiest lingerie she had, a minuscule bit of black lace and sheer silk, cut high on the sides and deep in the front and back. Then she paced the floor.

By midnight she was exhausted. She climbed into bed and fell into a fitful sleep.

A hand over her mouth awakened her.

"Don't scream."

Hawk! Her eyes adjusted to the darkness. He was

bending over her, dressed in the same buckskin shirt and jeans he had worn to the rally. The hilt of his knife gleamed in the darkness.

She reached for him, and his mouth slammed down on hers. They kissed without restraint and without mercy, as if he had just returned from war. The kiss went on and on until she was dizzy for lack of air.

At last he lifted his head. "I didn't mean to come back, Elizabeth."

"I know."

"I couldn't stay away. Not after seeing you again."

"I'm glad." She reached for the lacings on his shirt and began to pull them apart. Then she plunged her hand into the opening and pressed it flat on his chest. She could feel the hammering of his heart.

"I came through the tunnel so no one would see."

"Right now I don't care if the whole world sees."

"I won't endanger you, Elizabeth."

"Shhh." She put her hand over his mouth. "Don't talk. I don't want to waste a moment of our time together talking."

He shed his clothes quickly and joined her in the bed. The explosiveness of their passion threatened the antique bed. For one hour they loved, for two, and still they couldn't get enough.

When their passion was finally spent, Hawk spread Elizabeth's hair across the pillow and kissed her cheek. "You're mine," he whispered. And then he was gone.

Gladys eyed the clock the next morning when Elizabeth came into work.

"Will wonders never cease? You're ten minutes late."

"Traffic," Elizabeth said, marveling at how easily

she had become a liar. She had slept right through her alarm clock. Only by the grace of God and the early morning sun coming through a crack in her curtains had she been able to wake up at all. She had had to skip breakfast in order to get to work on time.

She hurried past Gladys in what she hoped was her usual manner and shut herself up in her office. Hawk had not said he would be back. That didn't matter. She would go to him—secretly, just the way he had come to her.

It was still daylight when she left work. Through a series of discreet phone calls and careful inquiries, she had found out where Black Hawk lived. Since his house had burned, he was staying in a small hunting cabin in the forest bordering his land.

She took the winding gravel road that led deep into the Chickasaw tribal lands to his ranch. It was a vast spread with well-kept fences and carefully groomed pastures. In all the time she had been back home, she had never driven out this way. She felt as she guessed a prisoner might who had just been released and was seeing the world without bars for the first time in years.

She drove slowly, but not so slowly as to call attention to herself. Black Hawk was careful not to mark them as a pair. She would be too.

After she had satisfied herself that she could find her way back in the dark, she turned onto a side road and made her way home.

When ten o'clock came, she dressed carefully, let down her hair, grabbed her gun, and made her way into her cellar. Black Hawk had shown her the secret passageway. She pulled aside the loose brick that hid the latch, then entered the tunnel. It was dark and damp. For a moment she felt as if she were suffocating.

She took a deep breath and plunged ahead. She would not be deterred. The prize was worth any sacrifice.

It seemed to be hours until she came to the end of the tunnel. Resolutely she climbed out and brushed the dust and twigs from her skirt. Then she tried to orient herself.

In the darkness all the trees looked the same. There were vast stretches of forest all around her, and there seemed to be no way out.

"Don't panic," she whispered. "You can do this."

She looked upward, located the moon, and began to track. There were no signs of Black Hawk. She hadn't expected to find any. He was not the kind of man who would leave a trail.

It took her thirty minutes to find his cabin. Keeping in the shadow of the trees, she made her way forward. She had almost reached the door when she heard him speaking from somewhere behind her.

"Don't move."

Slowly she turned toward the sound of his voice. "Hawk. It's Elizabeth."

He had her in his arms so fast, she thought a whirlwind had overtaken her. With one hand clamped firmly over her mouth, he carried her into his cabin, kicked the door shut, and set her on her feet.

"You could get hurt sneaking up on me like that."

"If that's your idea of a welcome, Hawk, it stinks."

His heart was still racing from finding her standing in his woods. He was in no mood for word games.

"Why did you come here?"

"Do you have to ask?"

"It's too dangerous. You shouldn't be here."

"I'm a big girl, Hawk. And I carry a big gun."

"How did you get here?"

"Through the tunnel."

Fury that she had risked her life to be with him boiled up in him. As he always did in moments of great passion, he resorted to the language of his ancestors. In the fluid, poetic tongue of the Chickasaws he cursed the Fates that had set this woman in his path, this woman who threatened to turn him away from his purpose.

"Please do me the courtesy of berating me in my own language."

"Elizabeth." He took her hands. "I don't berate you. I curse the Fates that threw us together."

"So do I." Her quiet dignity impressed him. "I don't want this any more than you do. I don't *need* this, Hawk . . . this wonderful and terrible connection between us."

"Neither do I. I won't allow you to become a part of my life."

They looked at each other, mute. Finally she broke the silence.

"What are we going to do about it?"

"I'm going to take you home. There are people who want me dead, Elizabeth. If they see you here . . . if they know what you are to me, they are likely to try to get to me through you. I won't have that."

"What am I to you, Hawk?"

It was another long while before he spoke. Elizabeth's skin tingled, and a lump rose into her throat.

"You are mine, Elizabeth. You came to my bed and I spilled my seed in you and you are mine."

At that moment, she wanted to be his. More than anything in the world, she wanted to deny her past, to forget its hard lessons, and to belong to this savage, passionate warrior. But she wouldn't ignore the lessons of her past, even for Hawk.

"No," she said. "I belong to no man."

He reached for her, but she stepped aside. "My way, Hawk. Tonight we will do it my way."

She took his hand and led him to a straight-back chair. "Sit here." He straddled the chair, and she walked away, her skirt swinging around her hips.

It wasn't her usual severe skirt she wore; it was a skirt of soft butternut suede that hugged her hips like a lover. A row of buttons ran from waist to hem down one side. A soft cotton jersey top, slashed low to reveal cleavage, skimmed her torso.

Elizabeth laid her gun on the bedside table. Then she turned to him and lifted her hair off her neck. She wet her lips with her tongue and began to sway.

Hawk was mesmerized by her hips. Their movement was so fluid, so smooth, they seemed to move separately from the rest of her body. A haunting, exotic music started from somewhere in the room, and it was a moment before Hawk realized it was Elizabeth singing.

He didn't recognize the song, but the lyrics were unmistakably erotic. Her lips swayed with the beat of the music, and she advanced toward him, slowly, ever so slowly. When she was so close he could smell her perfume but too far away to touch, she stopped.

"Do you want me, Hawk?"

"Yes."

"As you have never wanted another woman?"

"Yes."

"Tonight I am yours . . . and you are mine."

She stripped her shirt over her head and stood before him, with her arms held high. She was wearing a tightly-laced black bustier that left her breasts bare.

Bending down, she draped her shirt around his neck. Her breasts brushed lightly against his cheeks. He turned to capture them, but she stepped out of his reach.

"The patient man gets the prize, Hawk."

All thoughts of political battle and lurking enemies receded as Hawk leaned back to enjoy the sight of Elizabeth McCade. He loved danger, and right now he was playing the most dangerous game of all: He was flirting with a fatal attraction, one that threatened to bind him so tightly, he could never let go.

"Do you hear the music, Hawk?"

There was no music playing, but as Elizabeth began to move her hips again, he could almost hear the far-off strains of some mysterious, exotic melody. Holding her arms high above her head and thrusting her breasts proudly forward, Elizabeth increased the rhythm of her hips. The buttons on her skirt worked their way out of their buttonholes, one by one.

The soft suede skirt inched downward with the release of each button. Elizabeth's small waist came into view, and then her navel. She spun and swayed until she had bared her hips. A G-string of sheerest black lace covered them.

Hawk had to clench his fists in order to stay in his chair. The woman was a temptress, a sorceress, and he was under her spell.

Finally the last button was free, and the skirt slithered down Elizabeth's legs. Every nerve in Hawk's body was tingling, and his breathing was raspy as he sat watching her.

"I'm yours," she said, so softly, he had to strain to hear.

In one quick, fluid movement he lifted her and

carried her to his bed. Poised above her, he gazed down into her face.

"Where did you learn your sorcery, Elizabeth McCade?"

"From another man."

"I would like to thank him . . . and then to kill him."

"Once long ago so did I."

The need to know everything about her ripped through Hawk. He wanted to know who had taught her, where and when she had learned, and why she had wanted to kill the man. But overriding all that was his desire, a desire so great, it could no longer be controlled or contained.

"Elizabeth, you are in my blood. I'm drunk with you." Standing up, he cast his clothes off. Then he leaned down and caught her bustier with both hands. There was a tearing sound as he ripped it down the middle. Hungry for her, desperate for her, he ravished her with his mouth and his tongue. When the G-string got in his way, he tore it aside.

"You are my woman." He came to her then, entered her and became a part of her.

Together they were untamed and untamable. She brought out the savage in him, and he brought out the beast in her. It was a game for supremacy and control that lasted far into the night.

In the end, they lay in each other's arms, exhausted.

"I was not going to come to you again, Elizabeth."

"I knew that. That's why I came to you."

"I don't want you to come here again. It's too dangerous."

"Once I did a man's bidding." She raised herself on her elbow so she could see his face. "I will never again do what a man tells me to do, Hawk. I am my own woman. I am Elizabeth McCade, and I do what pleases *me*."

"Living in your shuttered house alone pleases you, Elizabeth?"

She sucked in an angry breath. "If you think you can drive me away with anger, Hawk, you're wrong."

She got off the bed and found her lingerie scattered on the floor. Then remembering that it was torn, she threw it aside and pulled on the rest of her clothes. He lay on the bed, watchful. She knew better than to think he was relaxed. Everything about him, from the tight line of his jaw to the tautness in his body, told Elizabeth that Black Hawk was a warrior through and through, always ready for battle.

Putting her hands on her hips, she faced him.

"I was cast aside once, Hawk. I will never be cast aside again. I will take what I want, when I want it . . . and then I will walk away." She pressed her right hand over her heart. "*I* will walk away, Hawk. Not you. Not any man. *I*, Elizabeth McCade, will do the walking."

Their gazes locked as their wills warred in mortal combat. At last, Hawk rose from the bed, magnificently naked.

Elizabeth watched him dress, taking pleasure in his body, in the fluidity of his movements, in his proud and noble bearing. His face was inscrutable when he turned back to her.

Without a word he held out his hand, and she came to him. He lifted her into his arms and carried her outside. He whistled softly, once, twice. Out of the darkness came a stallion so black, it blended with the night. In one fluid motion Hawk mounted, taking her with him.

They rode away from his cabin into the thick

woods, silently, swiftly, with the wind in their hair and the song of the night birds in their ears. When they reached the opening to the secret passageway, Hawk dismounted then lifted Elizabeth down.

"Sweet dreams, Elizabeth," he said. And then he was gone.

For the next few days, Hawk and Elizabeth worked tirelessly, desperately trying to forget each other. But it was impossible. They both burned with the same passion.

On a dark and moonless night, Hawk left his post high atop the bluff overlooking the city and turned his stallion toward the secret passageway. With a word, he sent the stallion home and climbed down into the crumbling tunnel.

He hurried along, aching with desire and burning with a need that would not be denied. Suddenly he heard a noise. Flattening himself against the wall, he drew his knife from his belt. The sounds came closer.

He strained his eyes into the darkness, and finally he saw it—a shadowy figure, making its way toward him. The figure came closer. It was a woman. Her long dark hair was swinging loose, and she had an unmistakably sensuous movement to her hips.

Elizabeth. His mind shouted her name, even as he remained pressed against the wall. She had been coming to him. In spite of his warnings, she had been making her way back to his cabin.

"Elizabeth." He said her name before he stepped into her path, for he had also recognized the gleam of her deadly Magnum. She ran into his arms, and he buried his face in her hair.

"You are the most stubborn woman I have ever

met." He took the gun from her limp hand and placed it on a stone jutting out of the wall.

"Hawk, Hawk." She ran her hands over his face, through his hair. "I tried to stay away."

"So did I."

For a moment they gazed at each other, trying to read expressions in the darkness. Then their passions unleashed, and they came together like a summer storm on the mountains. The sounds of their loving echoed in the dark, damp tunnel.

It was a tumultuous joining that left them both panting.

He reached out and gently touched her face. "Don't come to me, Elizabeth. I will come back to you."

Before she could reply, he left her.

"Hawk." She called his name but he didn't turn around. "Be careful," she whispered.

It was six nights before he came again. Each night Elizabeth waited anxiously, pacing her floors, wringing her hands. She had been keeping up with news of him through the media reports.

Gunshots had been fired at the barricade. No one was hurt, but reporters were saying that if a settlement was not reached soon, someone would be.

And that someone would be Hawk. Elizabeth knew it, for he was always at the front of the lines, always fearless, always the leader. Hawk would be the target.

The sixth night she was so exhausted from worry and waiting that she fell asleep in her chair with the lamp on and the television blaring.

When she woke up, she was sitting on Hawk's lap.

"Hawk." She ran her hands over his face, memorizing him. "How did you do that?"

"You sleep the sleep of the dead, Elizabeth. You always have."

"How long have you been here?"

"An hour."

"You wasted a whole hour letting me sleep?"

"It wasn't wasted, my beauty."

He laughed then, and Elizabeth thought it was the most beautiful sound in the world. Suddenly she knew: In spite of all her intentions, in spite of her past, in spite of her vows, she had fallen in love.

"Oh, Hawk," she whispered. She batted back her tears so he wouldn't see them. Hawk was not the marrying kind. She wasn't even certain she wanted him to be. She had trusted a man once; she didn't know if she could ever trust another, even if that man was a noble Chickasaw named Black Hawk.

He didn't see her tears, didn't hear the pain in her voice. He was too blinded by passion, a passion that claimed him as quickly as a brush fire consumes a parched forest.

He reached over and snapped off the lamp. There was no need to silence the television, for he had long since shut off that intrusive noise. He pushed aside their restraining clothing and took her in the chair.

He held on to her a long time, pressing her head against his chest so that she could hear the slow, steady beat of his heart. Then he kissed her once more and left.

Elizabeth gathered her wrinkled clothes about her and sat in the chair, staring into the darkness, wondering how she would ever survive unrequited love again.

Six

Elizabeth was weary and light-headed when she woke up the next morning. Fortunately, it was Saturday, and she didn't have to go to work.

She lay back in her bed and tried to convince herself that she had not fallen in love with Black Hawk, that it was merely lust she felt, but it was no use. She was too smart and too sensitive not to know the difference.

For the first time since she had come home she longed for a close friend, someone to talk to, someone to confide in. But her only friend was Hawk, and she could hardly go up to him and say, "Hawk, I love you." He had made it perfectly clear that commitment was not a part of the affair. Only passion.

"I guess I've lost again," she said to the stray cat who had come in during the night and was sitting in the basket beside the window, licking his paws. The cat switched his tail.

Elizabeth got out of bed and walked over to her dressing table. Her diary caught her eye. She reached for it, then drew her hand back. She was not the same woman who had once found solace in writing in a diary. Maybe Hawk didn't love her, would *never* love her enough to make a commitment. But he had taught her something: He had taught her the value of fighting for a better life.

She went downstairs and made herself a meal. After she ate, she felt better. Next she picked up her morning paper and searched it for news of the barricade. The Chickasaws were still holding the line. Since the gunshots the previous week, Tombigbee Bluff policemen had joined with the developers. A small sidebar to the main story told of a group of Chickasaw women printing pamphlets at the schoolhouse on the tribal lands, hoping to educate the public to their cause.

Elizabeth laid the paper down. She believed in the cause. She believed in protecting Tombigbee Bluff Forest from needless destruction, and she believed in the rights of the Chickasaw Nation to keep and protect the property deeded them under treaty laws dating back to the early 1800s.

A new resolve took hold of Elizabeth. Without even doing her dishes, she left the kitchen and got her purse, then climbed into her car. She was going toward the tribal lands, but this time it wasn't Hawk she was seeking: It was a different way of life. Elizabeth was tired of hiding, she was finished with safety. Elizabeth McCade was once again joining the mainstream of life.

The small school was nestled in a beautiful grove of oak and walnut trees. Three cars were parked outside a building marked "Administration." Elizabeth parked her car and walked boldly inside.

Seven women were bent over a table, discussing their latest endeavor at influencing public opinion, their soft voices blending together like music.

Apparently they didn't hear Elizabeth come in. They never looked up.

"It lacks something," a tall, slender woman said. "There's no fire in this copy, no passion."

"We could ask Black Hawk. He speaks with a tongue of fire."

The speaker was a young girl of about fifteen with two dark pigtails hanging down her back.

"No. He has too much to do already. And besides, he seems preoccupied of late. I sometimes wonder—" The slender woman broke off her speech as she turned and saw Elizabeth.

Slowly the rest of the group turned around and gazed at her. An uneasy silence fell over them.

Elizabeth walked forward, smiling. "Hello. I'm Elizabeth McCade."

The women in the group didn't speak, didn't move. Distrust was plainly written on their faces. Elizabeth was not deterred.

"I've come to help," she said simply, holding her hands palm up in appeal.

The slender woman, obviously the leader, moved forward and took her hand. "I'm Susan Mincohouma." She held Elizabeth's hand, studying her. "I am descended from a Chickasaw king who knew the value of allies outside our own people. If you are sincere, we welcome you." She released Elizabeth's hand and stepped back, her face hardening. "But if you are a spy sent by the people trying to take our lands, we curse you."

"I am not a spy."

"How can we be sure?" Susan said. The other women kept silent. "You are not one of us. I have never seen you at rallies, never heard your name. You are completely unknown to us."

Elizabeth took a deep breath. There was only one way she could prove to these women that she could be trusted.

"I am not unknown to Black Hawk." There was a collective gasp. "Black Hawk knows me; he trusts me." Elizabeth didn't say more, but waited, letting the women draw their own conclusions.

The other women began to whisper among themselves, but Susan stepped forward and took Elizabeth's hand once more.

"If Black Hawk trusts you, then *we* trust you. Welcome. We need all the help we can get."

"Just tell me what to do, Susan."

"What is your background?"

"A degree in English from Yale. I know more about writing than I do about printing. I have a car, and I have plenty of spare time. I'm no public speaker, but I'm willing to learn."

Susan handed Elizabeth a copy of the material she and the other women had been studying. "Read that, Elizabeth. It reads like the back of a pablum box. See if you can create a little fire."

Elizabeth thought of Hawk and smiled. "Creating a fire is what I do best."

She took the material and set to work.

Black Hawk burned with rage and fear, rage that Elizabeth had come to the tribal lands and deliberately exposed herself to danger, and fear that she would be hurt. He left his cabin and stood awhile in his yard, studying the dark to see if his enemies were watching. There was no sound, just the hushed movement of night wind among the pines.

He started through the woods on foot. It would take him longer to get to the mouth of the secret tunnel, but he would be less conspicuous that way. He moved quickly, darting among the trees. Before he plunged into the tunnel, he took one last look to see if there were watchers.

His foot loosened a stone and sent it tumbling

into the blackness. Black Hawk cursed silently in his ancient tongue. He didn't want even the tiniest sound to betray his presence at the tunnel.

He entered the tunnel and hurried toward Elizabeth's house.

Elizabeth was in her bedroom, brushing her hair.

He watched her for a while in secret. She was proud and strong, a woman of courage and spirit and fire. She was a woman a man would never tire of, a woman who would always delight and surprise a man. As he pressed himself against the wall of the hallway, pain slashed at his heart.

He had to let Elizabeth go. For her sake as well as his, he had to end their affair.

He reached for her, clamping a hand over her mouth and hauling her against his body. At first she was stiff and ready to fight, then, when she realized who it was, she melted against him, leaning her head back against his chest. He wanted to take her then. He wanted to enter her as the fire enters a lush forest, roaring and raging and burning everything in its path. He needed her, needed her passion, her wildness, her heady magic. He wanted to disappear in her and never have to come back to face the realities of a harsh and thoughtless world.

But that was selfish. What he had to do was convince her to stay away from him.

He turned her in his arms and tipped her face up with one hand.

"I can never touch you without wanting you."

She smiled. "I'm not refusing."

He searched her eyes, her face. He was hungry, starving for her. But he had to be strong.

"Elizabeth, why did you come to the tribal lands today?"

"How did you know?"

"Susan Mincohouma told me."

"Why?" Her temper flared. "Does she report all the doings of the women to you . . . or does she report specifically on me?"

"There are no secrets in this battle, Elizabeth. All my people report to me. I know everything that happens on Chickasaw lands."

"This has nothing to do with you, Hawk." Her voice softened, and she reached up to caress his face. "This was not a ploy to see you or to get close to you." She smiled once more. "If I want to get close to you, I have better ways of doing it."

She inched closer, her body suggesting another way. Hawk wrestled with temptation.

"Elizabeth." His fingers bit into her shoulders. "You must stay away. I don't want you involved."

"Why? You're involved. Why can't I be?"

"Things have been happening this week, bad things."

"What?"

"Two of my brothers have found butchered cattle on their ranches. There would have been some on mine except for the guard I keep posted. And my sister was run off the road in her car yesterday."

"I'm not afraid. You've given me courage, Hawk, the courage to leave my shuttered house and start living again."

"I know you have courage, Elizabeth. But you must choose another way. I'm a target. This violence is not random. It's directed at my family, the people close to me. I won't have you become a target because of me."

"It's not your choice. I believe in preservation of history and conservation of natural resources as much as you do. And I've decided to start doing something about it." She tilted her chin at a stubborn angle and glared at him.

Hawk knew that she meant what she said.

Elizabeth would not stop simply because he asked her to. She was that stubborn—and that brave. There was only one way to drive her off.

"It won't work, Elizabeth." He released her and stepped back, his voice hard and cold.

"What won't work?"

"This latest ploy of yours." She sucked in an angry breath and flags of color stained her cheeks. Hawk wanted to pull her into his arms and run his hands down her back until all the stiffness vanished, but he dared not.

"It's over, Elizabeth. What we had is over and done with."

"This is not about sex, Hawk. It's about pride and commitment and courage."

He resisted the urge to touch her. He couldn't waver now. Her life depended on it.

"It's about sex, Elizabeth, raw sex. You sought me out once at the rally. Remember?"

She clenched her hands into fists and stared at him.

"We're alike, Elizabeth. I know you as well as I know myself. We're two people ruled by our passions."

"Speak for yourself, Hawk. I'm in control."

"Are you?" He dragged her into his arms and slammed his mouth down on hers. She sagged against him. Then, as his tongue plundered her mouth, she heated up. Every fiber in her body became tight and ready, ready to explode.

He kept on kissing her, edging her closer and closer to the breaking point. Soon there would be no turning back, for him as well as for Elizabeth. Hawk pushed almost to the point of no return, then he let her go and stepped back.

"Are you, Elizabeth?" he asked, deliberately making his voice mocking.

"Damn you, Hawk."

It was what he wanted—her anger. He had done what he'd come to do. But he didn't feel noble and triumphant; he felt like a snake crawling on its belly.

"Stay away, Elizabeth. Stay out of my life and out of my bed." He had one foot already through the bedroom door when she called his name.

"Hawk!"

He turned, and there she stood, stripped of everything except a creamy white bustier, garter belt, stockings, and high-heel shoes. He gritted his teeth against the desire that swamped him.

"Do you think I will be abandoned again?" She moved slowly toward him, illuminated only by the glow of the bedside lamp and the soft gleam of white silk lingerie. "Do you think I'll let another man turn his back and walk out on me?"

"Elizabeth . . ." His voice was hoarse.

In a languorous movement, she lifted her hair off her head and let it filter slowly through her fingers until it was settled around her shoulders and over her bare breasts like a dark cloud. "Hawk . . ."

His resolve shattered. He closed the space between them in two strides and pulled her into his arms.

"Is this what you want, Elizabeth?" He lifted her up, and she wrapped her legs around him. He took one of her breasts deep into his mouth.

"Yes, oh yes."

Elizabeth McCade and Black Hawk unleashed a storm of passion that threatened to destroy both of them. There was anger and frustration and pain and deep, deep longing in their mating. And there was something else, something so strong and so beautiful, it could never be destroyed: There was love.

Elizabeth felt it well up inside her as she and Hawk said good-bye. Tears wet her cheeks and ran down the side of her throat, but she didn't make a sound. She concentrated all her powers on saying good-bye to the man she loved. Her way. This time Elizabeth McCade was the one saying good-bye, and she would be the one to walk away.

When their passion was spent, Hawk held her tightly in his arms without speaking. There was nothing more to be said. Finally he released her and walked away, back through the secret passageway that had brought him to Elizabeth. And now it was taking him away.

Elizabeth sagged against the door, resting her forehead on the jamb. Tears rained silently down her cheeks. She made no attempt to brush them away.

In the tunnel, Hawk stood with his head bowed. Saying good-bye to Elizabeth was one of the hardest things he had ever done. For the first time in his life he questioned his priorities. He was a warrior, and he would continue to fight all the battles that needed to be fought. But the victories would be hollow. Without Elizabeth, everything in his life would be hollow.

At last he made his way home. The victory was not yet his. There was work to do.

Elizabeth fought hard against depression after Hawk left. Her disastrous affair with Mark had changed her life. But her affair with Hawk had not been disastrous; it had been wonderful. And now it was over. She was determined that *this time* she would not run away and hide. *This time* she would get on with her life. And she would get on with her new causes. There was no way she would let Hawk or any other man tell her what to do. From now on, she made her own choices, and if those choices set her on a dangerous path, that was her problem. Not Hawk's.

On Monday at work she invited Gladys to lunch. They went to a small sandwich shop near the bank.

"Thank you for coming, Gladys."

"Why wouldn't I, I'd like to know?"

"I've been a virtual recluse the past seven years." Elizabeth smiled. "You can't say that I've been the friendliest person in the world."

"No. I can't say that, but you are one of the most interesting. You're a woman of mystery." Gladys leaned forward, propping her elbows on the table. "Do you have any idea how many rumors there are about you floating around the bank . . . and how many of the girls on the first floor would give their eyeteeth to know what we're talking about today."

"When we get back, Gladys, you can confirm the most exotic of the rumors, whatever they are."

"They say you led a secret life in Connecticut and that you lead a secret life here in Tombigbee Bluff."

"Yes. I turn into a witch on alternate Tuesdays and a vampire on weekends." Elizabeth said with a deadpan expression.

"You're a card, Elizabeth." Gladys laughed until she wiped tears from her eyes.

"Actually, I'm getting involved in the Chickasaw resistance."

"Good Lord. Isn't that dangerous?"

"I don't think so. Anyhow, some things are important enough to take a risk over, and I believe this is one of them."

"That leader . . . Big Hawk . . ."

"Black Hawk."

"Lordy, he's some kind of man. I wouldn't mind getting involved in the resistance myself, if I though he'd look at me twice."

Elizabeth squeezed her hands together under

the table. Black Hawk was out of her life. She had to remember that.

"If you're serious about helping, I'll take you with me tonight. I'm going back to the schoolhouse on the tribal lands to work."

"Shoot. I can't tonight. I've got a hot date. But how about the next time? I really would like to help. I'm not the fluff-head I sometimes pretend to be."

"Done." Elizabeth picked up the tab for both lunches, then turned back to Gladys. "I notice you knitting sometimes in the lounge. I wonder if you'd teach me."

"It's no big deal. I'd be glad to. But why in the world would you want to learn how to knit?"

"You mean, how will I ever have time, considering the exciting secret life I lead?" Elizabeth laughed.

"Something like that."

"I just feel the need for . . . a hobby. Something new in my life." *Anything,* she thought. Anything to fill the horrible, lonely hours now that Hawk was gone.

That night Elizabeth was bent over the antiquated copying machine at the schoolhouse when she heard hoofbeats. She felt as if an electrical current had passed through her body. *Black Hawk.* She pressed one hand over her pounding heart and tried to get herself back under control. Just because somebody was approaching on a horse didn't mean it was Black Hawk. There were bound to be many men who rode horses.

The door burst open, and Elizabeth spun around. There was Black Hawk, framed in the doorway, looking as dark and forbidding as a thundercloud. Without a word he strode directly toward Elizabeth.

She hoped he didn't see how disturbed she was. She had to be strong, strong against her love for Hawk.

"Hello." She smiled. "Isn't it a little late to come calling on a horse?"

"I told you not to come here."

"As you can see, I don't take orders."

His gaze swept the room. "Where are the other women?"

"They've already gone home. It's late."

"You stayed here alone?" His voice was like a clap of thunder.

"Obviously."

He grabbed her shoulders and hauled her up against him. A muscle worked in his tight jaw.

"Elizabeth . . . what am I going to do with you?"

She tipped her head back and challenged him with her dark eyes. "I think we've already done just about everything, don't you?"

He held on to her a moment longer, then let go. He was still unsmiling, but a spark of humor lit his black eyes.

"I liked you better when you stayed shut up in your house with the blinds drawn. At least you were safe." He stalked to the other side of the machine, scowling at everything in sight.

"That's because you like to be in control, Hawk. You like to be in charge." She stalked after him. When she was even with him, she lifted her chin and put her hands on her hips. "I won't be taken charge of, Hawk. You've declared a war that you can't possibly win."

"I have not declared war on you, Elizabeth."

"Yes, you have. When you came to my basement issuing ultimatums, you declared war."

They glared at each other, and the air became thick with tension. Color rose in Elizabeth's cheeks, and Hawk's breathing became harsh. Suddenly he hauled her to him.

"I wish all my enemies were as sexy as you, Elizabeth . . . and as easily vanquished."

His eyes were blacker than doom as he bent down and captured her mouth. It was a relentless kiss, a kiss that allowed no mercy. She fought hard against the feelings that threatened to swamp her—passion and need and a love so great she wondered why it wasn't written in blazing letters in the dark night sky. And finally, she could resist no more than she could deny her own name. With a soft sigh she surrendered.

Hawk's kiss became tender and so persuasive that both of them almost buckled to the floor. He slid his hands up her legs until he reached the top of her stockings. His fingers burned into her warm flesh.

"Hawk . . . no." Elizabeth pushed against him with all her strength. "I won't be manipulated with sex. Once I was . . . but never again." Her hands were shaking as she wiped them across her mouth.

Hawk stepped back, tension etched in his face and every line of his body.

"I'm sorry, Elizabeth. That was manipulative."

He hooked a straight-back chair with his foot and straddled it. "You aren't going to quit, are you?"

"No." She went back to the balky machine and started feeding papers in. "What's going to happen, Hawk?"

"Ultimately, we will win."

Elizabeth smiled. "Besides that."

"The mayor and his board are using the press to drum up support for the mall. Any time new jobs and additional tax dollars are mentioned, the public listens. Right now, that issue is obscuring the real one: The city doesn't own the land in question. The Chickasaws do."

"And the city still won't sit down with you and talk."

"No. They hope time will swing so much support their way that we will give up and walk away."

There was no sound for a while except the whirring of the machine as Elizabeth printed copies of her pamphlet. Suddenly she switched off the machine and whirled to face Hawk.

"I know a way to *make* them talk to you," she said.

"How?"

"Take me captive."

"What?" Hawk stood up so fast, his chair tipped over and crashed against the floor.

"If you had a hostage, you could force the mayor and the board to come to the negotiating table with you."

"Are you suggesting that I use you to fight this battle for me?"

"I'm not suggesting that, exactly. I wouldn't really be a hostage. But they wouldn't have to know that." She smiled, enamored with her plan. "It's perfect. I don't know why I didn't think of it sooner."

"No!"

"You don't have to roar."

"I will not hide behind the skirts of a woman."

"I'm not talking about *you*, Hawk. I'm suggesting you use me for the cause, for all the Chickasaws."

"It's cowardly. A warrior is never cowardly."

"You are the most stubborn man I've ever seen."

"You are the most impossible woman."

They came toward each other and stood toe-to-

toe. Elizabeth tipped her face up and Hawk bent down until they were almost nose-to-nose.

"I don't know why I lov—" She stopped herself just in time.

"What did you say?"

"I said . . ." She took a deep breath. "I don't know why I bother with you."

He studied her for a long time. And everywhere he looked, she felt the heat, almost as if he had touched her. But she remained staunch. She knew how to love and lose. He had taught her that.

At last he smiled. "You bother with me because you are Elizabeth McCade." He walked over to the table and picked up her purse. Then he opened it and pulled out her Magnum. "And because you carry a big gun."

"Yes, I do. And don't you ever forget that, Hawk. I can take care of myself."

She turned the machine back on and picked up a sheaf of papers. Hawk picked up the overturned chair and sat down. Elizabeth looked over her shoulder at him.

"That was your cue to leave."

"I'm staying."

"That's not necessary."

"Elizabeth, if you insist on doing dangerous things, I'll do my best to protect you. My only concern is that I can't make it a twenty-four-hour job."

Elizabeth was silent for a while, wishing for things she knew she couldn't have—Hawk in her bed, in her life, twenty-four hours a day. She studied him. He looked magnificent and noble and tired, very tired. She knew he was spending long hours at the barricade, keeping watch and keeping peace. It had to be physically and emotionally exhausting. Besides that, he was giving speeches, granting interviews, trying to persuade the city fathers to set up an official meeting for negotiations, and running his ranch.

Elizabeth switched off the machine. Her intention was to help him, not add to his problems. Quietly she gathered her purse.

"I really do appreciate your concern for my safety. Thank you for coming, Hawk."

"You're welcome, Elizabeth."

The moon was full and bright, clearly illuminating her car and the black stallion waiting patiently for his master.

Elizabeth started toward her car, then turned back to Hawk and put her hand on his cheek.

"Be safe," she whispered.

He covered her hand, pressing it hard against his flesh.

"Elizabeth . . . Elizabeth . . ." The pain in his voice broke her heart all over again.

"Kiss me, Hawk. One last time . . . and then go quickly."

He bent over her with the swiftness of his namesake and captured her lips. She clung to him, fighting the tears that pushed against her eyelids. She wouldn't let him see her cry. Not now, not ever.

As always, they kissed without restraint, without regard to the time or the place. And neither of them saw the watcher in the nearby forest.

Seven

Elizabeth spent an exhausting week, leaving work every day and going directly to one public function after another. She had put pamphlets in every willing hand in Tombigbee Bluff. And she had discovered that she had a small talent for rhetoric. On the previous night she had been asked to speak at the Rotary Club about her part in the Chickasaw resistance.

It was no wonder that when Saturday morning came she felt weak and queasy. She dressed, but the thought of food made her sick. She gathered her knitting and dragged herself downstairs. Switching on the television for company, she sat in the most comfortable chair in the den and began the tedious process of knit and purl.

She hated knitting. Gladys had patiently taught her the stitches, but Elizabeth had serious doubts that she would ever produce anything besides the long chain of yarn that resembled a crooked snake.

"If this ever becomes an afghan, it will be a miracle," she muttered. She gave serious thought to taking up a new hobby—painting, for instance. Although she had no artistic talent, she thought it might be therapeutic to take brush in hand and slash a white canvas with black paint. She would definitely use black, because that was the mood she was in lately.

Suddenly the television caught her attention. "We interrupt this program to bring you a special news bulletin. Fighting has broken out at the barricade." Elizabeth was on her feet. Yarn and knitting needles clanked to the floor.

". . . no details yet," the reporter was saying, "but there are unsubstantiated reports that the Chickasaw leader, Black Hawk, has been shot."

Elizabeth ran out of the room, leaving a trail of yarn and the television blaring. Her hands were shaking as she grabbed her purse and fumbled for the car keys.

She drove like a madwoman across town, ignoring all speed limits. When she reached the barricade, all she could see was mass confusion. People were running every which way. There was shouting and yelling, pushing and shoving.

She raced into the thick of the crowd. "Please . . . let me through."

An officer of the Tombigbee Bluff Police Department grabbed her arm as she tried to go under the ropes that cordoned off the area.

"You can't go in there, lady."

"I have to get through."

"Nobody gets through, lady."

"I *must*. I have to get to Hawk."

"Nobody is going to get to him now."

Elizabeth almost fainted. She clutched the officer's sleeve. "Is he . . ." Words stuck in her dry throat. The possibilities were too horrible to even think about, let alone speak.

Suddenly there was a thundering of horse's hooves. "Elizabeth, get back," Hawk yelled.

She broke free and ran toward him. He leaned

down and scooped her into his arms. The stallion never broke stride. At Hawk's urging, the stallion jumped the barricade and galloped off toward the forest.

Hawk didn't stop until they were deep in the woods. Then he dismounted, taking Elizabeth with him.

"Are you crazy?" He hauled her up against him. "Two men have been shot out there today. The barricade is no place for a woman."

"I thought you were dead." She sagged in his arms.

He pressed her close and began to caress her hair. She shuddered. Hawk rocked her gently, murmuring soft words of comfort in the language of his people.

They stayed that way for a long while, and gradually Elizabeth became calm. She lifted her head and gently touched Hawk's cheek.

"You're safe," she whispered. "That's all I want to know."

"Yes, I'm safe."

Even as he spoke the words, Hawk knew he was lying. He realized he was facing his greatest enemy: Love. Without his knowledge, love had crept in and lodged itself in his heart. He was in love with Elizabeth McCade. Standing there in the tranquil woods, he knew that he was his father's son, after all. Grant Hawk had been one of the greatest leaders the Chickasaws had ever known, willing to take up any battle for the betterment of his people—until he had fallen in love. After that, nothing mattered to him except Dovey and the many children they had, one after the other. Their story was almost legend among their people, how the Great Hawk had been tamed by a gentle Dove.

Love had weakened Grant, had caused him to lay down his shield and sword. With Elizabeth's hand touching his face and her dark eyes searing his soul, Hawk was tempted to do the same thing. But he had been bolder than his father, had made more enemies. Even if he were willing to divide himself between love and war, he would never expose Elizabeth to the uncertainty, the danger.

"What will happen now?" Elizabeth took a step backward, breaking all physical contact. Hawk wished the emotional connection were as easily broken.

"Today's violence destroyed any hope for a meeting between the Chickasaws and the city government. We will have to call for outside help."

"Who?"

"The U.S. Secretary of Native American Affairs. I had hoped to settle this dispute alone, but I can't risk further violence."

Elizabeth was so quiet, he thought delayed shock was setting in. He was reaching for her when she spoke. Quietly he withdrew his hand. It was best not to touch her. Touching her was more dangerous than facing that sniper with the Winchester.

"But until he comes . . ." Elizabeth bit her lip. It was a familiar gesture. He had seen her do it many times when he had first hidden in her house. She was fighting against strong emotions. "What will you do until he comes? The television reporter said there was shooting. Somebody is going to get killed."

"Fortunately the police had been at the barricade for days, trying to prevent just such a thing from happening. They caught the sniper."

"Who was he?"

"Apparently he was an independent radical. He denies any connection with the developers and with the city government."

"Is he the man who burned your house and tried to kill you?"

"It's too soon to know." She was biting her lip again. Hawk sought to reassure her. "I believe he was the one." He put one hand on her shoulder. "It's over, Elizabeth."

She lifted her chin and gazed deeply into his eyes. "Is it, Hawk?"

He hesitated only a second. There was double meaning in their words and both of them knew it. They were talking about more than the battle between the Chickasaws and the city; they were talking about their own personal battle, their affair that had burst into flames so quickly, it had almost consumed them both.

"Yes," he said. "It's over. I'll take you home."

"What about my car?"

"I'll send one of my brothers to bring it to you when I get back to the barricade."

He circled her waist, then stood looking at her. A primitive need rose in him, a need to lay her on the soft carpet of moss and claim her as his own one more time. He wrestled with temptation for a long while, then from the deepest reaches of his soul, he dredged up a sense of nobility. It would be selfish and unfair to take advantage of her that way. She wouldn't deny him: He knew her well enough to know that. But she might grow to hate him, and Hawk could never endure it if he earned the hatred of Elizabeth McCade.

He lifted her onto his stallion and mounted behind her. Then he set a swift course toward her home.

For the next few days the papers and the television were full of news of the battle at the barricade. The sniper, Graden Hogan, still denied all political connections. With him in jail, peace reigned, and the people of the city drew a sigh of relief. It had been a long, hot, insane summer, and they were ready for the soothing, cooling touch of sanity and of fall.

Elizabeth followed developments closely. The Secretary of Native American Affairs was scheduled to arrive soon. A quick settlement was expected.

Newspapers and television were her only contacts with Hawk. He didn't come to the schoolhouse or tribal lands anymore; he didn't come to any of the rallies she attended, or if he did, he slipped away quietly without her knowing; and he certainly didn't come through the secret passageway to her cellar. More than once she was tempted to make the journey herself. Especially late at night. Especially when she lay in her lonely bed with her body and her heart aching for Hawk.

But Elizabeth kept tight control. For the first time in many years, she was in charge of her life and of her emotions—until the middle of September when she awoke and began to count the days. . . .

She sat up in bed and pressed her hand over her mouth. "Oh, no," she said with a moan. "It can't be." She pulled the covers up to her chin and counted back to the day she had first seen Hawk, the day she had first kissed him, and the night she had first lain in his bed. Tears stung her cheeks. Her past was happening all over again.

Her hands were shaking as she pushed back the covers and got out of bed. She walked to her desk and picked up her diary. She rustled frantically through the pages until she found the ones she sought. Then she began to read.

The words blurred as all the pain of her past came back to her, doubled. Quietly she closed the diary and stared into space. How would she ever survive the coming days and months and years without Hawk? If only she could see him, if only she could talk to him. But she was too proud. He had made his position clear. "I don't want you in my life or in my bed." Elizabeth was alone.

The phone jarred her out of her stupor. It was Gladys.

"Have you seen the morning paper?"

"No." Elizabeth cradled the receiver against her shoulder and returned her diary to its drawer.

"You're spread all over it."

"Why? I certainly haven't done anything news-worthy."

"How is this for newsworthy?" Gladys's voice lowered an octave as she shifted into her dramatic mode. "And I quote the headline, 'The Lady and the Hawk.' There's a great picture of you and Black Hawk in a clench with the moon shining over your shoulder. It looks like the schoolhouse in the background."

Elizabeth gripped the receiver so hard, her knuckles turned white. "Who did this?"

"You know that brash new reporter . . . John What's His Name . . . the one who was always following us around when we distributed pamphlets, trying to sniff out a human interest story?"

Elizabeth groaned. Then she clapped her hand over the receiver so Gladys wouldn't hear.

"Elizabeth, are you all right?"

"I'm fine."

"You don't sound fine. You sound sick."

"No. This will all blow over." But she knew it wouldn't. It would never be over. Not now.

"I doubt that. He's done some pretty thorough homework. Does the name Mark Laton ring a bell for you?"

"Nooo. Not that too."

"'Elizabeth McCade has a habit of secret liaisons. Sources say she left Yale because of an illicit affair with Mark Laton, a professor who was married.'"

"What else?"

"There's a great picture of you and Black Hawk on that stallion of his, leaping over the barricade the day fighting broke out."

"Anything else about Mark?"

"No."

At least she could be glad for that much. Elizabeth took several deep breaths in order to get herself back under control.

"Elizabeth . . . is there anything I can do? Are you sure you're all right?"

"No . . . yes. I'll be fine, Gladys. Don't worry about me."

"I do, you know." Gladys's voice softened. "That was a dirty rotten thing to spread your private life all over the newspaper, but I'm not sorry you have Black Hawk. I've suspected all along that you had somebody wonderful in your life. I'm glad, Elizabeth."

"It's over. Hawk is no longer in my life."

"I'm sorry."

"Thank you, Gladys. You're a good friend."

"See you at work in a little while. I'll treat you to lunch, take the bad taste out of your mouth."

"Sure." Elizabeth forced some enthusiasm into her voice. Gladys was, after all, a good friend. She had no connection with the series of misfortunes that were befalling Elizabeth. "Great. See you later."

She hung up the phone then went into the bathroom and vomited. When she came out, Hawk was sitting on the edge of her bed.

"Good morning, Elizabeth."

She pulled her robe high around her neck and shivered.

"Are you sick?" He stood up, facing her.

"No. Just a little chilly. There's a nip to the air this morning." Turning her back to him, she sat at her dressing table and picked up her hairbrush. Then she began to brush her hair. She looked calm, even to herself. She hoped she was fooling Hawk. He towered behind her, reflected in the mirror in all his noble splendor. She felt sick all over again, sick that she didn't have him, sick that she couldn't talk to him, sick that she couldn't hold him.

"Have you seen this morning's paper?" he asked.

"Is that why you came?"

They stared at each other in the mirror. She heard the subtle change in his breathing, saw the light spring to life in the center of his dark eyes. She knew all the signs: Hawk still wanted her. At least she had that.

"Is Mark Laton the one?" Hawk had his hands on the hilt of his knife.

Suddenly Elizabeth broke. She was not noble and long-suffering and magnificent; she was merely human. She stood up and faced him with her fists clenched.

"How dare you come into my house and question me about Mark Laton. How dare you enter my bedroom without my permission. You have no rights, Hawk. None. You gave those up in my cellar a long time ago."

"You're right, Elizabeth. I gave up my claim to you."

His ready agreement made her even more furious. Dammit, he didn't have to give in so easily. Why didn't he fight for her? Why couldn't he want her enough to fight for her?

Her shoulders sagged, and all the anger went out of her. Hawk wouldn't fight for her because he was already fighting too many battles . . . and because he didn't love her. She might as well face facts.

"Will you please leave?" She put her hand on her forehead.

"I didn't come to fight with you, Elizabeth. I came to tell you that I'm sending my brothers to be your bodyguards."

"You're sending your brothers to be my bodyguards!" She felt as if she were in the middle of a crazy movie.

"Because of the newspaper story."

"There has been no violence since that man was arrested."

"I'm taking no chances. My youngest brother is with me now, waiting downstairs."

"You can't do this. You can't march into my house and take charge of my life."

"I'm not in charge of your life, but I *will* be in charge of your safety."

"Tell him to go home." Hawk was dreadfully silent, as silent as the cutting edge of a sword just before it draws blood. "I won't have him here. Nor any of your other brothers. I can take care of myself."

"You are willful, Elizabeth."

"You are arrogant."

They faced off across her bedroom, two stubborn people, both determined to win.

"We're just alike, Elizabeth. We've always been alike."

"No."

"No?"

"I'm a woman and you're a man."

Hawk smiled. "There was never any doubt."

His smile seduced her. She had to bite her lip and clench her fists to keep from reaching out to him.

"Please leave," she whispered.

"How can I go when I feel the danger to you? How

can I leave knowing that I'm the one who set it in your path?"

"I made my own choices, Hawk."

They faced off again, both as implacable as the red bluffs that bordered the city. Then Hawk came to her and tenderly cupped her face.

"Be safe."

"I will. I promise."

Black Hawk left her standing in the middle of her bedroom and went back down the stairs just as quietly as he had gone up them. Steel, his youngest brother, was waiting for him outside.

"You told her?"

"Yes."

"And she agreed to the bodyguard?"

"No."

Steel laughed. "I didn't think she would. From what Susan tells me, she's a very independent lady."

"You will guard her anyway."

"Look. I'm a young, handsome charmer with my whole life ahead of me. I have no desire to meet my fate at the end of a nickel-plated .44 Magnum. Especially if it's carried by a lady."

Hawk threw back his head and laughed. "She's tough, all right, but you will guard her, and you will be wise and discreet enough to stay out of her way so she doesn't suspect."

"Do you love this woman?"

Black Hawk had never lied to his brother. He considered it briefly, then rejected the idea as cowardly.

"Yes, I love her."

"Then why aren't you the one guarding her?"

"She must never know. She must never know that I love her." He turned a fierce face toward his brother. "I won't come to her again; I won't see her again. But you, my little brother, will keep her safe."

Steel started to say something else, but he knew his brother too well. It was useless to argue with the Hawk. When he made up his mind, nothing would stop him.

Elizabeth made it to work on time by skipping breakfast and by exceeding the speed limit. With her private life splashed all over the front page of the newspaper, what would one speeding ticket matter?

Tailing far behind in his beat-up little Chevy Nova, Steel Hawk was cussing.

"What does she think this is? The Indianapolis 500?" He said a few more words that his mother would have frowned upon, then pressed down on the accelerator in order to keep his quarry in sight. The Hawk would kill him if he didn't do this job right. And he was too young to die.

He saw the flashing blue lights behind him at the same time Elizabeth's car disappeared around a bend.

"Well, hell. Where's the justice?"

As the policeman walked toward his parked car, Steel brightened. He thought he would plead for a very large fine and then present it to his brother for payment. It would serve the Hawk right. Any man who refused to acknowledge his love for a woman like Elizabeth McCade deserved to be taught a lesson.

He rolled down the window and smiled at the officer.

"I'm just as guilty as sin . . ." He read the name tag. ". . . Officer Bradley. I'll bet I was doing seventy-five in that fifty-mile zone."

"Only seventy-two." The officer was young and friendly. He pushed his cap back from his forehead. "Going somewhere in a hurry?"

"No. Just chasing a pretty woman. If I were you, I'd throw the book at me."

"You would?"

"Shoot, yes. I drive like this all the time. I need to be taught a lesson."

"Well . . ." The officer surveyed Steel's beat-up little car. "It appears to me that a feller like you has all the problems he can handle trying to keep an old car like that running. I'm going to let you off with a warning this time."

"Hell," Steel muttered.

"What did you say?"

"I said, 'Help' at a time like this is most welcome. My sincerest thanks, Officer Bradley."

"You're welcome. Just watch it. There's been enough excitement in this town lately. We don't want any traffic fatalities."

"You bet." Steel shook Officer Bradley's hand, then set off down the road. Elizabeth McCade was long gone.

He hoped that she had been heading to work, and not to some out-of-the-way place where he would never find her. He didn't relish the idea of telling the Hawk that he had lost his woman on the first day.

Steel breathed a sigh of relief when he cruised by the bank and saw Elizabeth's car. She was safe, at least for the next few hours.

He found a parking spot that allowed a good view of her car, then left his jalopy and went to a music store to stock up on a fresh supply of tapes. If he had to spend the best days of his life watching after a woman who wasn't even his, the least he could do was keep himself well entertained.

Over the next few days, he learned Elizabeth McCade's habits. She had a strict morning routine that included stepping outside briefly for her paper. Steel, hiding in the woods that surrounded her house, enjoyed these early morning views of Hawk's woman. With her hair down and a loose robe wrapped around her, she was sensational. It was no wonder his brother loved her. The wonder was that the Hawk was not fighting for her. Surely no cause could be worth the price of this woman.

Watching from the woods, Steel saw Elizabeth McCade turn and look his way. There was a tenseness about her that alerted him. He ducked behind a tree, his heart hammering. He didn't want to face the Hawk's wrath if he was discovered. He waited, scarcely breathing, listening for sounds, for smells, for anything that would announce Elizabeth McCade's approach. Finally he heard her front door slam.

He slumped at the base of the tree and gave his brother a very sound cussing. Then he got up and continued his vigil.

By nine o'clock Steel realized that something was wrong. Elizabeth should have been out of her house twenty minutes before and on her way to work. It was not like her to be late.

By ten o'clock Steel was really worried. What could be the matter? Had someone sneaked into her house while he wasn't watching? Was she lying in a pool of blood even as he paced? He didn't even want to think about such a thing.

Forcing himself to remain calm, he began to rationalize. Perhaps she had called in sick. Or maybe this was her day off. He'd give her thirty minutes more, and then he'd go inside to see about her . . . and hope he didn't get caught.

He waited while the minutes crawled by. At ten-thirty he skirted the edge of her yard, staying in the cover of the trees. When he was behind her house, he ducked low and zigzagged a course toward her back door, using the cover of large bushes that had only recently lost their summer blooms.

Steel was no expert on breaking and entering, but he was not without skill. It didn't take him long to get inside Elizabeth's house. He stood in the kitchen, tense, waiting and watching. There was no sound.

Drawing his knife from his belt, he began a stealthy exploration. It took him fifteen minutes to discover the truth: Elizabeth was not there. She had spotted him and had made her escape.

He didn't know which he feared most: Elizabeth's peril or the Hawk's wrath. There was only one thing he could do. He resheathed his knife, got his car, and went to inform his brother.

Elizabeth hurried through the tunnel. After she had spotted the man in the woods, she hadn't even bothered to put her hair up. She had dressed and called in sick, which happened to be true. She had been dragging lately, and this morning she had felt especially exhausted.

There was no doubt in her mind who the man hiding in the woods was. He looked too much like Hawk for her to be mistaken.

She clenched her fists. "Damn you, Hawk. Damn you."

She was absolutely furious. How dare he try to run her life. Especially now. She was so mad, she hadn't even taken the time to get her gun. The danger was passed now. There had been no violence since that day at the barricade. The city had settled in to wait for the advent of the U.S. Secretary of Native American Affairs.

Elizabeth would be glad when it was all over. Then everything would settle back to normal. Everything except her own life. It would never be the same.

She stepped from the tunnel and brushed the dirt and twigs off her skirt. It was the same butternut suede she had worn to seduce Hawk. She figured some bit of perverseness had caused her to wear it. She wanted him to want her as badly as she wanted him—to want her and not be able to have her.

"Elizabeth McCade," she said aloud as she walked through the woods toward Hawk's cabin, "you have sunk to the lowest of lows."

There was no need to hurry. What she was going to say to him was best done in a cold, calm rage. She didn't want to be out of breath and practically fainting on her feet when she faced Hawk.

"Well, well, well. Looka here."

Elizabeth whirled at the sound of the voice. The man appeared out of nowhere and stood in her path, blocking her way to Hawk's cabin. He was short and barrel-chested, with bloodshot eyes and several-days growth of scraggly beard covering the lower half of his face. There was a strong smell of whiskey on his breath.

She pressed her hands over her stomach to still the sudden attack of nausea. She had to remain calm.

"Who are you?" she asked.

"Who am I? Who am I?" He spat onto the ground near her feet. Elizabeth forced herself not to cringe.

"Black Hawk's slut wants to know who I am." His laughter sent shivers through Elizabeth.

The man came toward her, his eyes wild and evil looking. "I ain't no Indian lover. That's for sure."

Elizabeth cursed herself for being unarmed. Hawk had warned her of the danger. Repeatedly.

And he had been right. She had made a fatal mistake in thinking that she was out of danger.

She would have to keep her wits about her. That was all.

"I have no quarrel with you." Elizabeth held her hand out, palm up, in a gesture of supplication. "Every man is entitled to his own views, and if ours differ that doesn't mean that we are enemies."

"Enemies? Enemies!" The man's wild laughter echoed through the woods. "Hell. We ain't enemies." He began to move toward her then, talking as he came. Elizabeth forced herself to stand still. She must not show fear. Perhaps if she didn't show fear, he would turn and walk away. "I'm the avenger. Yessir, that's what I am. I'm the avenger, and you're the victim."

She almost fainted. Even if she were well, she would be no match for this man. She turned and ran.

He lunged for her and caught her leg. She went down, screaming. Immediately she felt his dirty hand clamp over her mouth. Elizabeth struggled, kicking and scratching and biting. If she was going to be the victim, she would not be an easy one.

"Be still, slut." She sank her teeth into his hand and hung on. "I'm going to teach you a lesson or two."

The first blow landed in her stomach. Elizabeth fought and struggled until she was too weak to move. Gradually the forest faded and the sun got dim. She was vaguely conscious of her attacker standing over her, feet planted on either side of her body.

"What a tidy little present for that trouble-maker."

Elizabeth groaned as he picked her up. There didn't seem to be a spot on her body that he had missed. He carried her for what seemed like agonizing hours. She had no idea where he was taking her. Finally, as the pain got worse, she no longer cared.

Suddenly he dropped her. The hard ground jarred her body and rattled her teeth. Just before she blacked out, she heard her attacker yell, "She's all yours, Black Hawk."

Eight

Hawk was in his north pasture, supervising the loading of cattle for the market when he saw his brother coming. He shaded his eyes against the morning sun. Steel parked the car under an oak, bailed out, and started running.

It took Hawk about two seconds to read the alarming body language. He bent over his stallion and urged it into a gallop. When he was even with his brother, he wheeled in tight and leaned down low, shouting.

"What's wrong?"

"It's Elizabeth. I've lost her."

Hawk vaulted off his horse and caught Steel's shoulders. "What do you mean, you've lost her?"

"I think she spotted me this morning in the woods. When she didn't leave for work, I got worried. She's always so prompt."

Steel stopped talking, and Hawk realized he was gripping his brother's shoulders so hard that his own knuckles were pale. He released his brother. "Go on."

"I broke into the house a little while ago to check on her. She's not there. Her car is in the garage, but she's gone. . . . I'm sorry, Hawk."

112

"It's not your fault." Hawk forced himself to remain calm. Nothing had happened in days. There was no reason to believe anything had happened now. "Elizabeth is very strong willed. She probably spotted you, then called one of her friends to pick her up somewhere. She's probably at work right now, laughing about fooling both of us."

He wished he believed what he was saying, but he didn't. From the moment Steel had appeared, Hawk had known that something was terribly wrong. He felt it. It was almost as if he heard Elizabeth calling his name.

He vaulted onto his stallion. "Call the bank, Steel. See if she's there. Then meet me at my cabin."

"Where are you going, Hawk?"

"I know a place. . . ." The wind caught his words and carried them away as he galloped across his pasture and into the forest.

Elizabeth would have come through the tunnel. That's where he would start looking.

He rode hard and fast, and within fifteen minutes he was at the entrance to the tunnel. There were signs of her everywhere—footprints, broken twigs, even a strand of her long black hair caught in the low-hanging branches of a tree.

"Elizabeth." He didn't realize he had spoken her name aloud until he heard the mournful echo in the silent forest. Such a sense of forboding filled him that he almost wept.

He tracked quickly, following the signs. When he saw the other signs, he vaulted from his stallion and knelt on the ground. A man, a large one, had been in the forest this morning. He had been sloppy and careless. Cigarette butts littered the forest floor, and three empty whiskey bottles lay at the base of a pine tree.

A glacial cold descended over Hawk's soul, and a rigid control took hold of him. As he followed the parallel signs of Elizabeth and the man, Hawk was as forbidding and deadly as a stalking grizzly.

He was almost within sight of his cabin when the signs merged. His heart froze, and his breathing threatened to shut down. The signs were so clear, he could almost see the struggle. He knelt and came up with blood on his hands.

He lifted his face to the morning sky. "If this blood is Elizabeth's, I swear that there will be no hiding place for the man who did this."

Hawk saw her the minute he entered the clearing. Elizabeth was piled on his doorstep, one leg angled under her body, and her black hair spread across the dirt.

"Elizabeth!" He drew his knife and ran toward her in a zigzag pattern. If the man who had done this to her was still watching, Hawk wouldn't be an easy target.

When he reached her, he knelt down and cradled her in his arms. "Elizabeth . . . Elizabeth." She was dirty and bruised and bloody. His hands searched her body as he called her name, over and over. He felt a pulse. It was weak, but it was there.

"Hawk!" Steel called as he got out of his car and ran toward him.

"I did this to her, Steel."

"No."

"Yes. It might as well have been me." Hawk buried his face in her dark hair. "I couldn't stay away from her. My mind told me to stay away, but my heart wouldn't let me."

"It's not your fault." Steel spotted the note lying underneath Elizabeth's hip. "Here. Let's get her into the car. We've got to get her to the hospital." Under the guise of helping with Elizabeth, he palmed the note and stuffed it into his pocket. His brother didn't need anything else to worry about.

Steel drove like a maniac while Hawk held Elizabeth. His brother looked as if he had been carved from marble. God help the man who had done this to Elizabeth, Steel thought.

Hawk didn't want to leave her side, even when the emergency room nurses insisted.

Steel put a hand on his brother's shoulder. "There's nothing we can do now except wait."

It seemed like hours before the doctor came back to them.

"Which one of you is her husband?"

"Her husband?" Steel asked.

Hawk stepped forward. "Elizabeth belongs to me." The question he most wanted to ask was stuck in his throat.

"You're her next of kin?" The doctor turned his keen gaze on Hawk.

"She has no kin. She has only me." Hawk took a step closer. His control was beginning to snap. He wanted to grab the doctor's lapels and yell in his face, *Is she alive?* "I am responsible for her."

"She has a concussion, severe contusions, no broken bones, no internal bleeding."

"Was she . . ."

"Sexually molested? No. Thank God." The doctor played with his stethoscope as he faced Hawk. "She's had a very severe beating, but I don't think she will lose the baby."

"The baby?"

"You didn't know?"

"No. I didn't know."

"We'll monitor her carefully, of course. But at this point I think both mother and baby will be fine."

"When can I see her?"

"It will be hours before she wakes up, but you can go in now."

The doctor left, and Steel put his hand on Hawk's shoulder.

"Thank you for standing by me, Steel."

"That's what brothers are for."

"You can go home now."

"What about you?"

"I'll be here until Elizabeth awakens, and then I'll find the man who did this to her."

Steel squeezed his brother's shoulder and left the hospital. But he didn't go home, he went to see Sheriff Wayne Blodgett. If Steel had anything to do with it, the Hawk would never get his hands on the man who had attacked Elizabeth.

After his brother had gone, Hawk went directly to Elizabeth's room. She lay on the bed with tubes running out her arm. Her hair was spread upon the pillow, framing a face that looked unnaturally pale and still.

Hawk sat on the edge of the bed and took her hand. Elizabeth never stirred.

"Why didn't you tell me? Why didn't you tell me about the baby?"

He thought of all the ways they had loved, of all the times they had come together in order to produce the miracle that lay inside Elizabeth's womb. Joy and pride and love welled up inside him, and his spirit left the drab hospital room and soared like the hawk for which he was named. And then a great sense of sadness descended on him. How Elizabeth must have suffered, knowing she carried his child and believing he would not want it. He thought of her courage and her strength.

Had she known about the baby when he brought Steel to be her bodyguard? She must have.

"You have no rights," she had said. "You gave them up in the cellar."

And he had told her that he had given up his claim to her. Well, he had been wrong. He pressed her hand against his lips.

"I never gave up my claim to you, Elizabeth. Never." He leaned close and studied her. Sleeping, she looked so fragile, so vulnerable. It was hard to believe that the woman who lay on the hospital bed was the same one who had threatened him with a .44 Magnum.

"I have always loved you, Elizabeth McCade . . . and I always will."

Hawk held her hand between his and pressed them to his forehead, then he bowed his head in prayer. He didn't know how long he prayed, how long he stayed by her bedside, holding on to her hand. Time was no longer measured for him in minutes and hours but in the rise and fall of Elizabeth's breathing.

"Hawk?" Her voice was soft and weak as she tried to lift her head.

"Shhh. Don't move. I'm here."

She squeezed his hand. "Don't leave me."

"I won't."

Her eyes closed, and she was asleep once more. Hawk left her bedside and paced the room. Soon . . . soon Elizabeth would be fully awake, and he would find the man who had done this to her.

Sheriff Blodgett wasted no time after Steel came to him with the note and the story of the attack on Elizabeth McCade. "Black Hawk, nothing of yours is safe from me" the crude note had said.

"It's the same handwriting as the note we found the night his house burned," Wayne told Steel as he stooped in the woods, gathering evidence. He bagged and labeled the whiskey bottles, the cigarette butts, and minuscule bits of thread and cloth. "I'll lay you odds it's the same man."

"What about the one already in jail?"

"He's not the one who burned Hawk's house. And he's certainly not the one who did this." Wayne straightened up and rubbed the small of his back. "I'm getting too old and fat for this job."

Steel laughed. "No, you're not. You're still the best criminal investigator in this country." He became serious. "Can you find this man before the Hawk does?"

"Not if Blackie gets a head start on me . . . but I'll try."

"I intend to see that he doesn't."

"Sounds like you are two peas in a pod."

"I've never thought so before, but maybe we are." Steel grinned. "I wouldn't mind that. The Hawk has always been a hero of mine."

"Mine too. But don't tell him I said that."

Elizabeth didn't awaken again until morning. Hawk was sitting beside her bed, holding her hand, when she stirred.

"Hawk?" Her voice was stronger.

"I'm here, Elizabeth."

She stared at him for a long time without speaking. He couldn't read her face, but he saw the pain in her dark eyes.

"Why are you here?" She pulled her hand out of his, and her voice was cool and distant.

"You asked me to stay."

"Now I'm asking you to go."

"Elizabeth . . ."

"Please . . . just go. I don't want to see you."

Hawk was torn between obeying her and arguing with her. In the end he decided it was best to obey, at least for the time being. Elizabeth was in no condition to be upset.

"I'll go, Elizabeth, but I'll be back."

He walked quietly out of the room, then stood outside her door, leaning his weary head on the door frame. He looked up when Steel approached.

"How is she?"

"Much better."

"You look beat. Why don't you go home and get some rest?"

"I don't have time to rest."

Steel put a hand on his brother's arm. "Don't do it, Hawk."

"I must."

"Let the law handle this."

"I will avenge Elizabeth."

"Hasn't there been enough violence already, Hawk? Won't you be sinking to their level if you go after this man in your present frame of mind?"

"Don't try to talk me out of this, Steel. There are some things a man must do." He put his hands on Steel's shoulders and gave him a weak smile. "Don't worry, little brother. Everything will be fine."

"Let me go with you."

"No. I need you to stay here and watch over Elizabeth. Don't let anyone in this room who doesn't belong here."

"I guess you told her I'd be doing this."

"No. And don't let her see you. Elizabeth is a proud and stubborn woman."

"Sounds as if you've met your match." Steel grinned.

"Just give me your keys, Steel. I'm taking your car back to the ranch."

Steel knew he had lost. He handed the keys to his brother. There was no stopping the Hawk now.

He found a chair and brought it back to Elizabeth's door, then he sat down and began his vigil.

Hawk found his quarry by nightfall. The trail hadn't been hard to follow. The man had been careless and foolhardy—and now he would pay.

Hawk sat atop his stallion in the long shadows of the hills and watched the man making a campfire. From the way he moved, Hawk decided he was drunk.

Rage blinded Hawk for a second, and he felt himself getting out of control. Never had he been out of control when he fought a battle. He made himself sit quietly until he could gain his composure. When he faced this enemy, he wanted to be as cold and deadly as the razor edge of a sword.

He waited until the man was squatting beside his fire, far away from his Winchester, then he rode boldly into the circle of firelight.

"Good evening, Walter."

Walter Martin stumbled backward and fell onto his backside. Hawk urged his stallion closer, so close, his horse was almost stepping on Walter.

"What do you want?" Walter's voice had gone high with fear.

"What do you think I want, Walter?"

"I . . . I didn't do it."

"Didn't do what?"

"That woman of yours . . . I wouldn't do nothin' like that."

"Like what?"

"Well . . . you know . . ."

"No. Tell me." Hawk dismounted so fast, Walter barely had time to flinch. Then he caught the man's collar and jerked him off the ground. "Tell me, Walter . . . what did somebody do to Elizabeth McCade?"

Walter swallowed hard and stared at his captor.

"Did they ambush her, Walter? Did they defile her with their dirty hands? Did they bruise and bloody her and jeopardize her baby? *My* baby? Did they, Walter? Did they?"

Hawk never raised his voice, never changed his expression, but at that moment Walter Martin would sooner have been in a den of rattlesnakes than facing the wrath of Black Hawk.

"Oh, please. Please don't hurt me."

"Why not, Walter? Why shouldn't I do the same things to you that you did to Elizabeth?"

Walter's mouth worked, but no sound came out. Watching him, Hawk suddenly felt his blood lust vanish, and in its place was a cold and deadly determination. With one hand he reached for the rope looped around his saddle horn.

"What are you doing?" Walter whined as Hawk twisted his arms behind him and tied him up.

"I'm taking you in, Walter. You're not worth the time and effort it would take to give you what you deserve."

Relief made Walter's shoulders sag. Hawk finished trussing him up, then slung him across the back of his stallion.

"Assault and battery, attempted murder, arson." Hawk named possible charges as he mounted. Walter Martin had been the one with a Winchester the night Hawk's house had burned. His had been the voice calling out in the forest: "I got him." Hawk was confident that at last he had caught the ringleader of all the plots against him. Whether Walter had been motivated by hatred of the Chickasaws or hatred of him personally, Hawk didn't know. And he didn't want to know. It was best not to probe Walter's sick, twisted mind, best to let the law have him and get on with his life.

"I think they will keep you for a long, long time,"

Hawk added as he headed toward town with his quarry.

Elizabeth lay in her hospital room in the dark. She had not seen Hawk since early morning, since she sent him away. She pressed her hands over her flat abdomen.

"Don't you worry, little one. I'll take care of you. I'll take good care of you."

One tear inched its way down her cheek, and then another. Her movements were angry and determined as she wiped them away. There would be no tears this time. She would be strong. Women alone *had* to be strong.

Her door opened, and in walked Hawk. Elizabeth squelched her quick surge of hope. She didn't believe in fairy tales anymore.

"Elizabeth." Hawk came toward her bed but stopped just short of taking her hand. The small omission made her feel lonelier than a thousand good-byes. Elizabeth clasped her hands tightly together and prayed for strength.

"Black Hawk." She acknowledged him with a nod of her head, being careful to use both his names. "My lovers call me Hawk," he had said. Well, she carried his child, but she was no longer his lover.

"I caught the man who did this to you."

"You caught him?" She fought hard to keep from trembling. She would show Hawk no weakness.

"Yes. His name is Walter Martin, and he's now in the hands of the law."

"I'm glad. Thank you, Ha . . . Black Hawk."

She saw his eyes darken. Hawk didn't miss a thing. But if her attempts at formality bothered him, he didn't show it. Damned his implacability.

"For you, Elizabeth, I would have followed him to the gates of hell."

"Thank you for stopping by to report. I'll feel safer now that he is behind bars."

Hawk moved closer to her bed. She clenched the edges of the sheet until her knuckles were white, praying he wouldn't touch her, knowing she could never be strong if he did. When he was so close she could see the lines of fatigue etched around his eyes, he stopped.

"You are healing rapidly, Elizabeth."

"Yes."

"You are a strong woman. That's good."

"Yes, I'm strong." Unconsciously she put one hand over her abdomen. Hawk saw the movement but didn't comment. "Please leave now."

"You took care of me once, Elizabeth. I want to take care of you."

"I don't need you."

"I need you."

"I'm sorry. I'm not that strong. I'm not strong enough to handle anybody's feelings except my own. All I know is that I want to get through this by myself and get on with my life."

His eyes were very dark as he bent over her swiftly and caught her face between his hands. "Your life and mine are intertwined, Elizabeth."

"No," she whispered, even as her heart said yes.

He kissed her with such tenderness, she almost changed her mind. Then the hard lessons of her past came to her, and she turned her face away.

"Please go."

"I'll leave. If that's what it takes for you to get well, I'll leave. But I'll be back. When you're strong again, I'll be back, Elizabeth McCade. I promise you that."

The door closed behind him, and Elizabeth stared at the wall. Hawk had once said he was a man driven by his passions. Would he be making such passionate promises to return if he knew she was carrying his child?

Hawk sent his brother home and took the watch outside Elizabeth's door. Even though the man who had attacked her was behind bars, Hawk had to be certain Elizabeth was safe—not only Elizabeth, but the baby, his baby.

"You can't stay here round the clock," Steel protested.

"I'll leave here only for one thing, to meet with the Secretary of Native American Affairs. Inform me when he arrives, then come back and take my watch—and don't argue with me."

Steel had been about to do just that. He shut his mouth and did as the Hawk asked. No, *commanded.* The Hawk didn't ask anything; he gave orders.

When Steel left, his brother was sitting in the chair with his back to the wall and his eyes searching the hall.

Elizabeth was making a rapid and remarkable recovery. The doctor and all the nurses who passed through her door told Hawk so. They also informed him when she was sleeping. At those times, he slipped into her room and sat at her side, sometimes holding her hand, sometimes tracing her face with his fingers, sometimes even lying beside her on the bed, holding her in his arms.

As always, she slept the sleep of the dead. She never even knew she had her own personal guardian angel. Though Hawk never considered himself in those terms. All he knew was that he had to protect the woman he loved, protect her . . . and then win her trust, for without trust there could be no lasting love.

The day of Elizabeth's release neared, and Hawk consulted Gladys in the hallway.

"You've been a faithful friend, Gladys."

"So have you, Blackie. I'm sorry for these circumstances, but I'm glad we got a chance to get to know each other. I don't know why she won't see you."

"Does she speak of me?"

"No. I don't understand that. I talk about all my old flames, but Elizabeth acts as if you don't even exist."

"She's a very proud woman." Hawk couldn't keep the pride from his own voice.

"I call it cutting off your nose to spite your face."

"No. Elizabeth is strong. She's always been strong."

"Thank goodness for that, or else she might have been here much longer."

"Are you going to take her home tomorrow?"

"Yes. I promised you I would, and I'm not about to back out, even if I have to hog-tie her and drag her to the car. There is no point in her trying to do everything by herself, and I told her so." Gladys patted Hawk's hand. "Don't you worry now. I'll get her home safe and sound, and I won't say a word about you planning the whole thing."

"Thank you, Gladys."

Late that night while Elizabeth slept, Hawk entered her room. He stood for a while, just inside the doorway, studying her. Her color was back, and she had only faint signs of bruising.

He walked to the bed and bent over her. With one finger he traced the line of her body from breast to thigh.

"You are a woman of fire, Elizabeth McCade," he whispered.

Then he lay down beside her and took her in his arms. She sighed softly and wrapped her arms around him. "Hawk?" she murmured in her sleep as she rested her cheek in the curve between his neck and shoulder, and snuggled close.

"You are my woman. Mine."

Nine

Elizabeth woke up in the middle of the night with the strong sense that she was not alone. For a moment panic gripped her. Without moving her head off the pillow, she slid her hand slowly under the covers and toward her night table. Only when she felt the cold hilt of her gun did she feel truly safe.

In one quick movement she sat up, bracing herself against the headboard and pointing her gun into the semidarkness.

"Don't move or I'll shoot," she called out.

"Elizabeth, you're safe. Nobody is going to hurt you."

Her eyes adjusted to the darkness, and she found the man to go with the voice. He was sitting in an easy chair on the other side of the room. She snapped on the light and laid down her gun.

"What are you doing in my bedroom, Hawk?"

"Watching over you."

His dark eyes lit in the center as he watched her, and she was suddenly conscious of her skimpy red lace gown and of what his gaze was doing to her body. She pulled the covers high around her neck.

"I don't need you here, and I don't want you here. Please go."

"Your body says you want me here."

"Damn you, Hawk."

He got up and started toward her.

"Don't," she said, holding up her hand. "Please don't touch me. I can't be strong when you touch me." He kept on coming.

"Night after night I touch you while you sleep."

She shivered, but it wasn't fear that made her react; it was pleasure. The thought of Hawk's hands on her body made her weak, almost weak enough to forget their past, forget the baby, forget everything except the quick, hot passion bursting to life inside her.

"How long have you been here?" she finally asked.

"Since you came home from the hospital. I have come here every night for two weeks, Elizabeth."

"Why? I'm safe. You caught the man who attacked me."

Hawk sat on the edge of her bed. She felt his body heat as his hip pressed close to her thigh. She inched away.

"Yes, I did. He won't ever hurt you again. I promise you that."

"Then why are you here? I'm out of your life and out of your bed. Remember?"

"You will never be out of my life, Elizabeth. You carry my baby."

She sucked in her breath.

"How did you know?"

"The doctors at the hospital told me." He leaned over her, his face fierce. "Did you mean to keep it from me, Elizabeth?"

"It's my body and my baby."

"It's *our* baby." Hawk's voice became gentle. "I was waiting for you to fully recover before I talked to you. In fact, I had meant to talk to you in the morning, but since you're awake . . ."

He smiled, and her heart melted. When her Hawk smiled, it seemed as if the whole world must be smiling too. Only . . . he was no longer *her* Hawk. She bit her lip, hard.

"We will be married. I'll rebuild my house. You can help me with the design. There will be a special room for this baby . . . and plenty of room for all the ones who come after him."

"Him? *Him?* Elizabeth tried to control the fury in her voice. She jerked herself out of Hawk's grasp and scooted to the other side of the bed. "That's just like you to start giving orders." Hawk's gaze was roaming her body, and she could feel his desire reaching out to her. She jerked the covers high over her breasts and glared at him.

"Do you think all you have to do is declare that this baby—my baby—will be a boy, and God will sit up and listen? Do you think all you have to do is mention marriage, and I'll come running? Well, you're sadly mistaken. I am Elizabeth McCade, and I'm in charge of my own life, thank you very much. When I marry, it will be for the right reasons, not because some Chickasaw warrior wants to claim his son."

"Elizabeth . . ." He came across the bed and pulled her into his arms. Her resistance was only token, and she knew it. He was Hawk, and she was his woman. No matter what the future held for her, she would always want him, always respond to his touch. "It's not like that." Hawk caught her face and forced her to look at him. "I love you, Elizabeth . . . I want you."

"No . . ." she whispered as his hands slid slowly across her shoulders, taking her straps with them. "You're just saying that . . ." He bent down and brushed his lips across the tops of her breasts.

". . . because of the baby." The covers rustled as he leaned over and snapped off the light. "I can't . . . I won't," she murmured as he pulled her down and began to suckle her breasts.

"Hawk . . . Hawk."

The fire that only Hawk could ignite blazed through Elizabeth, and she lost all control. Weeks of wanting him, of needing him, made desire burn all the brighter. They came together in a sweet, hot explosion.

They loved as they always had, with single-minded intensity and magnificent creativity. They loved as they always had . . . and yet, they loved differently. There was an added element of tenderness, a fine edge of caring that cut through all the passion like a bright and shining sword.

Around them the night shadows lifted and a faint glow of pink crept into the room. As release came, Elizabeth and Hawk called out to each other. And then he held her in his arms, caressing her hair and murmuring over and over, "I love you, I love you, I love you."

Elizabeth didn't believe him. She wanted to. How desperately she wanted to. But the lessons of her past had been hard, and the things Hawk had told her had been specific. He was a warrior. He was ruled by his passion: That much was clear. But he was committed to one thing and one thing only: the Chickasaw cause. She had known that from the beginning. And she had accepted it.

Only now . . . with Hawk's baby growing inside her womb, the acceptance did not come easily. She ran her hands down the length of his bare back and up again. She wouldn't trade the last few hours with him for anything. But she wouldn't repeat them. She couldn't. Not and remain strong.

They fell asleep wrapped in each other's arms. Elizabeth allowed herself that one last pleasure, for she knew that only too soon the morning would come.

He was waiting for her downstairs when she got up.

"I made you breakfast."

"Please, no. Even the smell of food in the morning makes me sick."

"I'm sorry. I didn't think of that. I guess I'm not used to being a father-to-be."

The words came to him so naturally that she was almost fooled. He even looked like a contented father-to-be, standing in her kitchen over a skillet of scrambled eggs. But she knew better. She forced herself to be realistic.

"Black Hawk, about last night . . ." The minute she had said his name, he had tensed.

"Yes," he said quickly. "About last night." He loosened his grip on the skillet and came to her. Before he could touch her, she turned away.

"I love you, Elizabeth."

"You don't have to say that just because I'm pregnant. Reality doesn't make me fall apart anymore."

"What we had last night—"

"—was magnificent passion," she said, interrupting him. "It was a beautiful way to say good-bye once more."

He grasped her shoulders and turned her back to face him. "Elizabeth, I didn't mean to let passion overcome me. I had intended to earn your trust first, to prove my love to you."

"Look, Hawk. The baby is yours. There's no doubt about that. And I won't be selfish. I'll let you see him . . . or her. But I don't want any false pledges of allegiance that you can't and won't keep. It's not fair. It's not fair to me or to you."

"This is not a false pledge. This is not a pretty speech motivated by my desire to claim my son."

"I wish I could believe that, Hawk. But I can't."

He took small encouragement from her familiar term of endearment. Gently he urged her closer until her head was resting on his shoulders. Then he began to massage her back.

"My dear, stubborn Elizabeth. I'll prove my love to you."

"It won't work."

"Why?"

"I've learned the hard way, Hawk. A woman never forgets the hard lessons of experience." She lifted her face to his. "And I know you. Fighting is in your blood. This land battle will be over soon, but there will be another. Some grand and worthy cause will capture your attention, and you'll feel the lust for battle again." She pulled out of his arms and stood back, looking at him. "I won't be the cause of you staying at a safe distance, watching from afar while others take the chances and face the danger."

"I make my own choices, Elizabeth."

"Precisely." She whirled around so he wouldn't see the gleam of tears in her eyes. "You didn't choose to conceive this baby."

"I chose you. Pregnancy is always a possibility when there is passion. Especially when there is a passion such as ours." She heard the smile in his voice, but she was not seduced. "Elizabeth, I love you," he added softly.

She turned back around so she could see his face. "How long have you loved me, Hawk?"

"Probably from the time I saw you standing in your cellar proudly facing the unknown with a big gun."

"How long?" She thrust out her chin and dared him to make up a lie.

"I realized I loved you the day you came to the barricade, the day of the shooting."

"But you waited until now . . . until you found out about the baby to say anything about it." He started to speak, but she held up her hand. "Please. Please, don't say anything that will embarrass both of us. I know why, Hawk. I don't fit in with your lifestyle. I didn't fit in then, and I don't fit in now. You are a warrior, not a family man."

"Elizabeth, I will fight for you. But I must know my enemy. What terrible thing happened to you that keeps you from my arms?"

"Let it lie, Hawk."

"I cannot. I will not. Look at me, Elizabeth." He tipped her face toward him. "Don't you know that I would never hurt you? Don't you know that I would never leave you?" His hands caressed her tight jawline. "Tell me. Trust me, Elizabeth."

"I can't." She twisted away from him. "I'm leaving now. When I come home from work, I don't want you to be here."

She jerked up her purse, then turned for one last word. "I won't keep you from seeing this baby, Hawk, but I will keep you out of my bed."

He watched her leave. Then he quietly cleaned up the kitchen. He had never expected such resistance. If he thought too much about it, he might even convince himself that Elizabeth was right, that he was offering marriage only for the sake of the baby. But he knew it was not true. Perhaps the baby was the catalyst that had thrust him on this course of marriage, or perhaps the attack on Elizabeth was the thing that had made Hawk see how precious she was to him. For whatever reason, he knew that he could not endure a life without Elizabeth. And now it remained for him to find a way to convince her of his love.

After he had cleaned the kitchen, he went back

to the bedroom and sat in a chair beside the window to think. Elizabeth's exotic fragrance hung in the air, and the strong sense of her presence permeated the room.

"Elizabeth, why do you resist me so?" In his great agony, Hawk spoke aloud. And then his gaze fixed upon her diary. It lay on her bedside table, closed and locked.

He walked across the room and picked it up. What were the hard lessons of Elizabeth's past? What terrible things had happened to her that made her refuse to acknowledge or even consider a future with him?

He turned the diary in his hand. The temptation to read it was great. Perhaps if he understood her better, he would know how to break down her defenses.

Hawk laid the diary down. He would never violate Elizabeth's privacy that way. There was only one thing to do—find the man who had betrayed her, and then he would find the truth.

When Elizabeth got home she knew Hawk was not there. The house had an empty feeling that echoed in her heart.

"So much for undying love," she muttered as she climbed the stairs.

She was more exhausted than she had expected to be. She supposed the combination of pregnancy and a recent hospital stay had sapped her energy—that, or a broken heart. Did people die of broken hearts?

She walked into her bedroom, pulling off her jacket and her skirt as she went. As she stretched across the bed, she saw the note propped on her bedside table.

"I will be back," he had written in a bold hand. "I promise you that. Hawk."

Elizabeth pressed the note to her lips, then she folded it and slipped it inside her diary. She wondered if all the important events in her life would eventually end up between the pages of a locked diary. In her present mood, she thought so.

Luck was with Hawk. Mark Laton was still teaching at Yale, and he was willing to talk.

On the long flight north, Hawk tried to imagine what the man would look like and what his own feelings would be at seeing the man who had taught Elizabeth the art of love.

"Is something wrong, sir?" a passing flight attendant leaned down to ask.

Hawk loosened his grip on the seat handles and relaxed the muscles of his face. "No. Everything is fine."

"Good." The flight attendant smiled. Maggie, her name tag said. "We like all our passengers to be comfortable. Enjoy your flight, sir."

The only thing enjoyable about the flight was that it put him closer to achieving his goal. All in all, he'd rather have been on a horse. He fought the crowds at Kennedy Airport, then rented a car and drove to New Haven.

Mark Laton was waiting for him at the appointed place, in front of the towering Gothic structure on Yale's Memorial Quadrangle. Although the autumn air was much nippier in Connecticut than in Mississippi, Hawk preferred to meet this adversary out of doors. He believed it would give him a home court advantage.

Mark Laton was smaller than Hawk would have guessed, and much older. What had Elizabeth ever seen in such a man? Involuntarily Hawk's hands curled into fists, then he forced himself to relax. He *must* not let his passions control him this time. Too much was hanging in the balance.

"Professor Laton." Hawk sat on a bench without extending his hand. He might have used subterfuge to get this interview, but he was no hypocrite.

"Professor Black Hawk . . ."

"Just Black Hawk."

"I can't tell you how flattered I am that you would come all the way from Mississippi to see me."

"The paper you did on the Boethian influence on the Clerk's Tale is well-known. Every scholar of Chaucer should read it."

"Indeed they should. Boethius's *Consolation of Philosophy* is just as relevant today as it was then."

The man was pompous and very susceptible to flattery. The sooner Hawk dealt with him, the better. He stood up so he would tower over the professor.

"At one time or another, all of us deal with adversity." Hawk gave the professor time to preen and get comfortable, then went in for the kill. "How did you deal with Elizabeth McCade?"

Mark Laton jerked his head back as if he had been slapped. Then his eyes narrowed.

"Are you another one of those damned newspaper reporters?"

"No. This is personal. I am Black Hawk, and I will have answers."

"But you said you were a professor . . . that you taught Chaucer."

"You made that assumption yourself. I merely talked about Chaucer."

"This is unconscionable." Mark Laton stood up to leave, and Hawk caught his collar. Mark looked like a worm caught on a hook.

"I am in a violent mood," Hawk told him. "If I get answers, I might restrain myself."

"Put me down."

"Only when you start to talk."

Mark took Hawk's measure, then his resistance crumpled. "What do you want to know?"

"Everything."

Mark sank back onto the bench and told how he had seduced the brightest student in his class. Hawk sat through Mark's tale of introducing Elizabeth to the ways of love. He saw Mark only dimly through a red curtain of rage.

Mark embellished the story, sliding his gaze sideways at Hawk to see how much punishment he could inflict.

"Enough." Hawk's voice rang out like a herald of doom. "Tell me why she left."

"Because I wouldn't marry her." Mark puffed out his chest and scored another point. "She loved me, you see."

"Did you love her?"

"No."

Hawk caught Mark's shirtfront and hauled him close. "You lie. No man could possess Elizabeth and not love her."

Hawk fought a long, hard battle for control. Finally he eased his hold. "Elizabeth told me that she once wanted to kill you. If you don't tell me the truth, I might oblige her by doing the job myself."

"It happened a long time ago." Hawk waited. The man was finally going to speak the truth. Hawk could sense it.

"She came to me after class one day. I could tell that she was unusually excited. Her cheeks wore the blush of the roses that climbed the lattice outside the building. She waited until all the other students had gone, and then she sat in a front row seat, facing my desk. I remember how prim she looked, how virginal. At that moment, I wanted her more than I had ever wanted any woman in my life."

Hawk was as still as death. *Don't let passion control you now*, he told himself. *Not when the truth is within reach.*

"She told me she was pregnant." Mark paused for breath, wringing his hands. In the telling, the sins of his past had come alive once more. He felt like a very old man.

"I panicked,". Mark continued. "I opened the desk drawer and pulled out my wedding ring. 'How can I marry you?' I said. 'I already have a wife.' She went very pale. I thought she was going to faint. I felt sorry for her, but I knew I couldn't give her any hope. My job, indeed, my very life here at the university was at stake. 'Surely you knew,' I said. 'Nobody can be that naive.' But she was. I could tell. She had never known I was married." His voice trailed off, and he became silent.

"What happened next?" Hawk prompted, his voice lashing out like a whip.

"I guess I really did love her. . . . For at that moment I toyed with the idea of running away with her, of chucking my job and divorcing my wife and setting up another life with Elizabeth McCade." Mark sighed. "But I didn't. Instead I laughed at her. 'You've made two terrible mistakes,' I said. 'Your first was in trusting me, and your second was in getting pregnant.'"

Suddenly Mark's shoulders slumped, and he sat staring into space.

"What did Elizabeth do?" Hawk asked.

"She stayed on here, but she dropped out of my class. Of course, I steered clear of her. I couldn't continue our secret liaisons after that."

Hawk refrained from remark. Nothing he could

say or do would be adequate punishment for a man like Mark Laton.

"I guess she finished her degree. There was talk about her around Yale. She became sort of a recluse," Mark added.

"What happened to the baby?"

"I don't know."

"She carried your child, and you don't know what happened to it?"

"It was not my responsibility. I made that perfectly clear to her."

"Killing you would be too merciful." Hawk stood and looked down on his adversary. "I think living with that guilty secret must be the worst punishment you could have."

Mark looked stricken as he glanced up at Hawk. "You have no idea what a relief it is to finally tell someone about this. I guess it's been gnawing at my conscience for many years."

"Is there more?"

"No. I've told you everything." Mark stood up and faced Hawk like a man. He even squared his shoulders. "Will you keep my secret?"

"Only the three of us will ever know . . . Elizabeth, you, and I."

"When you see Elizabeth, tell her I'm sorry."

Hawk didn't want to mention this man's name to Elizabeth. He didn't want her to know that Mark Laton still existed. But a rational side of him said that there could never be healing without forgiveness.

"Maybe you should tell her yourself."

"Perhaps I should." The color came back into Mark's face, and Hawk saw a flash of nobility that would have attracted Elizabeth so many years ago. "I suppose it would do me no good to offer my hand."

"No. Nothing has changed between us."

"Perhaps you can answer a question now? What is your interest in Elizabeth McCade?"

"She is my love. I will protect her and love her for the rest of her life . . . and when she reconciles her past, I intend to marry her."

Elizabeth was amazed at how easily Hawk had walked out of her life. She hadn't seen him in almost a week. His absence brought memories of another time, another pregnancy, another man who had also walked out on her.

No, she said to herself as she entered her front door and carefully placed her purse on the hall table. That wasn't fair. Hawk was nothing like Mark, *nothing.*

Taking her time, she removed her jacket. It seemed that the only way she could hold herself together these days was to do everything deliberately and methodically. If she held her life in a tight pattern, perhaps she could keep control.

She reached up and tucked a pin back in her hair. Loose ends. She hated loose ends.

"Take the pins out, Elizabeth. I like your hair free."

Her head jerked at the sound of the voice, and she spun around. Hawk was leaning in the doorway leading to her den, looking handsome and lethal.

"What are you doing here?"

"I told you I'd come back."

He closed the small space between them in three strides. When he was standing in front of her, so close his jeans were touching her thighs, he reached up and began to take the pins from her hair. She didn't move; she could scarcely breathe.

When all the pins were out, he laid them carefully on the hall table, then put both hands in her hair. The heat from his hands made her scalp tingle.

He didn't speak, he just stood there staring down at her with eyes as dark and unfathomable as the bottom of an ocean. The tingling sensation spread from her scalp to the rest of her. It was like wildfire. Her veins pulsed with the heat; every vulnerable spot in her body burned with it. Desire swept through her, hot and fast. She closed her eyes against its onslaught.

Hawk knew. She could tell by the tenor of his breathing and the way his hands tightened.

There was a deep murmuring sound, like distant thunder in the mountains. It seemed to be coming from the very bottom of Hawk's soul, but Elizabeth was too far gone with passion to know or to care.

Suddenly he lifted her and carried her through the kitchen and down the cellar stairs. She could hear the sound of her own heart beating in her ears. Hawk entered the passageway, and still Elizabeth didn't speak. Her mind told her to protest, but her heart said be still.

When they reached the mouth of the tunnel, Hawk carefully handed her out. His black stallion was waiting. He mounted, taking her with him, then wrapped her in a blanket that was draped across his saddle horn. The wind whistled in her ears as the stallion galloped through the forest.

Hawk was taking her captive. She didn't know where he was taking her, and she didn't care. All she knew was that at that moment she was his and he was hers. And if that made her weak, then she was only human. She would be strong tomorrow.

They rode for a long time, climbing high into the

hills, winding through trees turned scarlet and gold by the paintbrush of autumn. Elizabeth felt the steady thrum of Hawk's heart against her back as she leaned on him. It felt good to lean on Hawk.

When they reached the highest point on the ridge, Hawk dismounted and carefully helped her down. He caught the edges of the blanket and drew her close. She could scarcely breathe. Pent-up desire shimmered in his eyes and tightened his body. Any minute now she expected he would cast the blanket to the ground and pull her down onto it. Could she resist? Now, after letting him take her captive and bring her heaven-only-knew where, could she still resist him? She bit her lower lip.

Hawk cupped her face, tipping it upward, so their lips were almost touching.

"I want you more than I've ever wanted another woman. Now . . . here on this bluff . . . my body cries out for you, is in agony for the kind of love that only you can provide. Only you, Elizabeth McCade."

He tenderly traced her cheekbones and the full shape of her lips. She sighed and tried to remain staunch.

"I want to spread my blanket on the ground and enter you. I want to possess you. I want to soar with you until both of us are crying out with pleasure." His hands tightened. "Then I want to spill my seed in you, just as I did this summer when I made you mine."

"No," she whispered.

"Yes. You are mine, Elizabeth. You will always be mine. I will follow you to the ends of the earth if that's what it takes, but I will have you . . . forever."

"Please, Hawk . . ."

He pulled her into his arms, turning her around so her back pressed against him. She could feel the tension in his body.

"What do you see, Elizabeth?"

"I see a stretch of forest, clean and beautiful, untouched by human hands."

"You see your future."

"Where are we?"

"Deep in Chickasaw tribal lands." He held her without speaking for a long while. "I want you to be a part of my life, Elizabeth. I want these to be your lands too. I've already made you my woman; now I want to make you my wife."

"The baby—"

"—might have opened my eyes," Hawk said, interrupting her. "But he has nothing to do with my love for you, with my desire to spend the rest of my life with you."

"I can't." She twisted around, and there were tears in her eyes. "Oh, Hawk, I can't. Don't you see? Right now while our passion is still bright and hot . . . while the idea of being a father is new to you, you think marriage is what you want."

"It is."

"I *know* you, Hawk, perhaps better than anyone else. I know the passions that control you." She turned away and gazed across the vast reaches of forest once more. "There will always be a cause that sets you aflame, a battle that needs a commander. Something inside you would die if you didn't have those things, Hawk." She faced him once more. "I won't be the cause of your discontent."

His fingers pressed deeply into her flesh as he cupped her face.

"I will change my lifestyle."

"No. . . . Right now perhaps you think you will, but you won't." She traced his lips with one finger.

His tongue wet the soft pad, then began a small, seductive movement. She quickly withdrew her finger. This time she would not get sidetracked by passion.

"You've given me a lot, Hawk—a beautiful summer of passion, the courage to take up my place in the community again, this baby." She paused, pressing her hands possessively over her womb. "From now on, my life will be what I make it. I won't run away, I won't shut myself into a shuttered house, and I *won't* be persuaded by a lethally passionate man on a black stallion."

"I want you, Elizabeth. I need you. I love you."

"I have never had any doubts that you wanted me, Hawk. But passion is not enough."

"Elizabeth . . ."

"Don't you see?" She held her hands stiffly at her side. "I put my trust in a man once. I can't . . . I'm not ready to do that again."

Hawk walked away and stood with his back to her. He looked every inch the noble savage as he gazed fiercely out across his ancestral lands. A small part of Elizabeth died at the thought of not having him in her life.

"You like to be in control of things, Hawk. I can't let you take control of my life—no matter how I feel about you."

"How do you feel about me, Elizabeth?"

She drew the blanket around her. Suddenly she felt the chill of October creeping into her bones.

"I have never wanted a man as much as I want you. I lie awake at night dreaming of the way you kiss me, the way you hold me, the way you touch me. My body longs to be slave to yours, even as my mind says no." She opened her hands and held them up to him. "I love you, Hawk."

"And yet you would deny us a chance because of

him." Hawk stalked toward her and gripped her shoulders. "I won't *let* you, Elizabeth."

"See? That's just what I'm talking about. You like to give commands." She drew out of his reach. "Well, I was a slave to love once. I won't be again."

"I am not Mark Laton." Hawk's voice thundered with anger. "I will never turn away from you the way he did. I have never lied to you or betrayed you."

She sucked in her breath, and her face got pale.

"And I would certainly never deny my child."

"How did you know?"

He reached for her hands. "He told me."

"You've seen him?"

"Yes. I flew up to talk to him."

"You had no right." She jerked her hands free and banged them against his chest. "What happened to me was private. It has nothing to do with you."

"It has everything to do with me." He pulled her into his arms and pressed her head against his chest, gentling her with his hands. "I had to know the enemy, Elizabeth. How can I ever win a battle if I don't know the enemy?"

"He's not *your* enemy, he's mine."

"He's sorry. He told me to tell you that."

"Sorry? Sorry!" She jerked her head up. "Does he think that makes up for all I went through. He's sorry!"

"Shhh, shhh . . ." He held her tightly, caressing the tension from her body. "It's over, Elizabeth. The past is over and done with."

She shuddered once, twice. The past *was* over and done with. That had been another time, another man, another child. Gripping Hawk's shirt, she gazed up at him.

"Don't you want to know what happened to the baby?"

"My only concern is *you*. I had to know how Mark Laton hurt you in order to know how to heal you."

"You can't make up for him, Hawk." She pulled herself out of his embrace and walked away. "I was young and scared and alone. At first I thought about . . . going to some back-street doctor. But I couldn't. It was *my* child. Flesh of my flesh. So I decided to have the baby. Other women supported families without a husband. I could too."

Drawing the blanket tightly around her neck, she turned back to face him.

"I never got a chance to find out if I could. I miscarried before anyone even knew I was pregnant. Mark was spared the embarrassment of having an illegitimate child."

"I'm sorry, Elizabeth. If I could erase your past and take away your pain, I would."

"You can't. Please take me home."

"I brought you here for a purpose, Elizabeth. I wanted to get us both away from a place that had any memories. I wanted you to see the ancestral lands from this viewpoint. I wanted you to know the kind of heritage our child will have."

"You can show the child when he is old enough. I won't stop you." She started toward the stallion. "I'm leaving. You can stay if you like."

He caught her around the waist and lifted her into his arms. "I will not let my child grow up without a mother *and* father, without a sense of family."

"How do you plan to get me to the altar, Hawk? By force?"

"If necessary."

Being in his arms again, her passion rose, bright and strong. Would there ever be a time when she would not desire the father of her child? She didn't think so, not if she lived to be a hundred. She would always want Black Hawk, always long to be in his arms, in his bed.

"Please, Hawk . . ." she whispered.

He leaned down and tenderly brushed his lips against hers. "I want more, Elizabeth, much, much more. But I'm willing to wait. I'm willing to wait until you can trust me, can trust in our future together." He mounted the stallion, taking her with him. "You will come to me, Elizabeth. And until then, you will feel my presence, you will know that you are mine."

"I won't come."

She thought he smiled, but she couldn't be sure. The dark descended on them as they made their way down the bluff and back toward home. This time, Hawk didn't take her to the tunnel. He rode boldly up to her door and carried her inside. Before he set her back on her feet, he gripped her chin and forced her to look at him.

"I took the long way home so people would see us together. There will be no doubt in Tombigbee Bluff that you are mine, that the baby you carry is mine. Don't think I will let you go, Elizabeth. Every time you look up, my stallion will be at your door."

"But you will never be in my bed."

She thought he was going to kiss her. He leaned so close, she could see the lights in the center of his dark eyes, could feel his warm breath fanning her cheek. If he kissed her there in the hall where they had shared so much passion, she wasn't sure she could be strong.

Finally, he released her. Arranging the blanket around her shoulders, he smiled. "Keep this. I want to know my blanket covers you at night." He started toward the door.

"Wait." She jerked the blanket off and held it out, but he kept on going.

Her hand trembled as she released the blanket. It landed on the floor in a rainbow of color. Elizabeth started up the stairs toward her bedroom. She was halfway up before she turned and went back for Hawk's blanket.

Ten

Elizabeth slept with Hawk's blanket covering her. When she woke up the next morning, the brightly colored Indian blanket was the first thing she saw. She lifted it to her face. It smelled of wool and saddle oil and pine needles and some indefinable masculine scent that was distinctly Hawk's.

She got out of bed, folded the blanket, and put it on the top shelf of her closet. Then she shut the door. But she couldn't shut Hawk out of her mind so easily. What was he doing now? Was he lying in his bed, magnificently naked, or was he already fighting the battle for his Chickasaw tribal lands?

She went outside and got the morning paper. The headlines announced the arrival of the U.S. Secretary of Native American Affairs. "The Chickasaw leader, Black Hawk, will be meeting with Robert Newton today," Elizabeth read.

She carried the paper inside and sat down at her kitchen table to finish reading about Hawk.

The reporter had done his homework well. He told of Hawk's long history of clashes with the city government. He outlined the reforms Hawk had brought about. There was a picture layout of the new recycling plant that had been built because of Hawk. There were interviews with various citizens who told how their lives had changed because of him, how they had become aware of the world they lived in and the need to preserve it.

Hawk's brother Steel dubbed him a "Warrior of the Nineties." He called his brother courageous and noble.

Elizabeth folded the paper and set it aside. Hawk was all those things—and more. How easy it would be for her to become starstruck, to follow him blindly, all the way to heartbreak. Just as she had Mark Laton.

She was pouring her second cup of hot tea when the phone rang. It was Gladys.

"Hi, I'm planning a big social outing on this wonderful Saturday. Shopping and a sinfully rich treat at JP's afterward. Want to go?"

Elizabeth started to decline, then thought better of it. She wasn't going to become a recluse again.

They spent most of the morning shopping, then settled into a booth at the back of JP's and ordered banana splits. When Gladys was deep into her whipped cream and chocolate, Elizabeth decided to share her secret.

"Gladys, I have something to tell you."

"I hope it's momentous. Life is getting so dull around here, I could use some shaking up."

"I'm pregnant."

"You're what?"

"I'm going to have a baby."

"Well, congratulations." Gladys reached across the table and squeezed Elizabeth's hand. "I guess there will be a wedding real soon, huh?"

"No."

"No?"

"I will raise the baby alone. Black Hawk has his life and I have mine."

Gladys settled back into her side of the booth, her mouth pursed. "How does he feel about this?"

"He says he wants marriage."

"He sounds like a sensible man to me."

"I won't trap him this way."

Gladys caught her hand. "Elizabeth, he loves you."

"How do you know?"

"I met him when you were in the hospital. Did you know he stayed outside your door round the clock? Did you know that every time you slept, he went inside and sat beside your bed, holding your hand and agonizing over you?"

"No. You didn't tell me."

"He forbade me to."

"He's good at giving orders."

Gladys released her and leaned back once more, squinching her eyes in deep concentration.

"He asked if you spoke of him, Elizabeth." Elizabeth didn't reply. "His heart was breaking. He wanted to be with you openly. He wanted you to need him, to want him."

"He wanted his child, that's all."

"How can you be so sure?" Elizabeth turned her face away. "What if you're wrong?" Gladys persisted. "Have you thought about that? You'll not only be throwing away your own chance for happiness but your child's chance for a full-time father."

Gladys tucked a big bite of whipped cream and chocolate in her mouth and swallowed in grim silence. Elizabeth toyed with her fork.

"Elizabeth McCade, I've never questioned your judgment, but now I have serious doubts about it. Blackie is a good man, a decent and noble man.

And I think I know enough about the male species to recognize a prize when I see one."

"I'm not denying that."

"Look, Elizabeth . . ." Gladys relented and reached over to pat her friend's hand. "I guess I came on a little strong. What you do is your business."

"Thank you, Gladys."

"And you have my full support. I want you to know that. I'll help you knit some little booties and bonnets. Shoot, I'll even knit a little christening dress. I want my goddaughter to be the best dressed little girl in Tombigbee Bluff. I can just see her now—Sophie Gladys Hawk."

"Your first name is Sophie?"

"Yes."

"Sorry to disappoint you, but it's a boy."

"How do you know?"

"Hawk says so."

That night Elizabeth dressed for bed and lay down on her cool white sheets. She glanced at the empty pillow next to her and sighed. What if Gladys was right? Was she throwing away her chance for happiness?

She lay for a while longer, then she got up and went to her closet. Reaching onto the top shelf, she hauled down Hawk's blanket and returned to her bed. Wrapped in its softness, she fell asleep.

Hawk found her that way. He stood beside her bed, staring down at her. Her black hair lay like silk against the intricate pattern of blues and reds and yellows.

Quietly he sat down and pushed the blanket aside. Elizabeth was wearing a sheer white teddy that hugged her body. He traced his fingers over her breasts. They were already showing signs of her pregnancy, the nipples enlarged and turned a dusky rose. He bent over and pressed his open mouth over her right breast. She sighed. Even in sleep she responded to his touch.

Hawk wet the silk until it was clinging to her tightened nipple. Then he slid his hand down her abdomen, cupping the small protrusion that was his child.

"Why must you be so stubborn, Elizabeth?" he whispered, moving his hand lower until he was covering her intimately. She smiled in her sleep.

Hawk wrestled with the temptation to enter her while she was still asleep. She would never deny him. Of that he was sure. Her passions were as strong and deep as his own. He took her nipple into his mouth once more, while his hand gently caressed her through the silk.

When his control was almost to the breaking point, he straightened up and pulled the blanket back over her. "Sweet dreams, my beauty."

She stirred. Stretching languorously, she sighed, then she opened her eyes.

"Hawk?"

"Hello, Elizabeth."

She looked at the luminous dial on her bedside clock.

"It's eleven o'clock, and all you say is 'Hello, Elizabeth.'"

"I can say more." He sat beside her. "I can *do* more. It's up to you, Elizabeth."

"Why are you here?"

"To check on you. To make sure you are safely tucked in bed and getting your proper rest."

"I won't be foolish, Hawk. I want this baby as much or more than you do." She sat up, pulling the blanket with her. "Why are you out so late? You should be getting your own rest. You look tired."

"I've just come from a meeting with Robert Newton and the city fathers."

"How did it go?"

"We've won, Elizabeth. There is no way Tombigbee Bluff can take Chickasaw lands, no matter how many tax advantages the mayor can think of."

"I'm glad, Hawk."

"It's over, Elizabeth."

"This battle is; there will be another one."

"Yes. I don't deny it." He took her hand and lifted it to his lips. "But I can handle it, Elizabeth. Tonight I realized that my life has been very one-sided. As I sat in that boardroom with all those officials, my mind drifted. I thought of you, here in this bed, and I wanted to be here with you, *in* you, touching you, loving you. I've been so caught up in causes that I've missed the things that are most important: love, family, friends."

"You were always good at speeches, Hawk. And very convincing."

He smiled at her. "I'm going to make some changes. I'm going to create the proper balance of work with play, of causes with family."

She didn't say anything, and he leaned down to kiss the top of her head.

"Sweet dreams, Elizabeth."

He didn't look back as he left the room. The door closed silently behind him.

Elizabeth put her hands to her hot cheeks, and the blanket slid downward. Only then did she realize that the front of her teddy was damp. She looked down at herself. Her nipples were peaked and straining through the damp silk.

"Hawk." She pressed her hands over her breasts. Hawk had touched her, had pressed his mouth over her while she slept. A great longing filled her, and a tear slid down her cheek. She wrapped her arms around herself and rocked back and forth on the bed, murmuring his name over and over.

She didn't see him again for a week. Although she knew she should have been relieved that at last he was letting her manage her own life, she felt uneasy and restless and even rejected. She figured it was her pregnancy that was making her so cranky.

"Some changes you've made, Black Hawk," she muttered to herself as she dressed and set about her Saturday morning chores.

With dust rag in hand, she descended on the room next to her bedroom. It was high time to think about fixing up a nursery. She removed a fine coating of dust that always seemed to collect in empty rooms, then dragged a chair over to the window and climbed up. The first thing to go would be the ratty old curtains.

Suddenly she felt strong hands around her waist. "What are you doing?" Hawk roared as he lifted her out of the chair.

"I was taking down curtains until I was so rudely interrupted."

"You will not jeopardize my baby by climbing on top of furniture." He looked at her as if she were out of her mind. If she hadn't been so mad, she would have laughed.

"I was not climbing on furniture; I was merely standing on a chair."

"If you want somebody to stand on a chair, call me. I'll come stand on a damned chair for you."

"I won't be calling you every time I want some little thing done. Turn me loose."

"Why?"

"So I can take these curtains down. I don't want the baby to have to look at the drab old things."

"My baby will be in the crib of his grandfather in his very own room out at the ranch."

"At the ranch?"

"You can decorate his room any way you like."

"You don't have room in that cabin for a baby . . . and anyway, he won't be there. He will be with me."

"Well, at least you're finally admitting you carry a boy." Hawk stalked across the room and jerked a blueprint off the chest of drawers. Then he spread it across the floor. "This will be our new house. Construction starts Monday. *Both* of you will live there, Elizabeth." His fierce gaze challenged her to deny him.

Elizabeth faced him with her hands on her hips. "I will not take orders from you, Hawk."

"All right." He tossed the blueprints onto the chest of drawers. "I won't argue with you about living accommodations. If you prefer to live here, that's fine with me. I'll move my things in. I can run my ranch from here."

"You'll move in?"

"That's what I said."

"I let you move in once and look what happened."

He smiled. She went to the window and gazed outside. The stray cat was worrying a mockingbird perched in a wild cherry tree. It was funny how everything in her life could be so changed and the outside world still looked the same.

She felt Hawk's hands on her shoulders. "Look at me, Elizabeth," he said gently.

She turned to face him. He brushed a strand of hair back from her temples, then slowly took the pins from her hair. It fell in a dark curtain around her shoulders.

"I always picture you like this . . . with your

hair down." He pressed his lips into the pulse point at the side of her neck. "You taste good, Elizabeth."

"Oh, Hawk . . ."

"I've waited for you." He unfastened the top button of her blouse and traced the tops of her breasts with his lips. "I've waited for you to call . . . to come to me."

"What we had, Hawk, was temporary insanity." He still kissed her breasts, and her breathing became raspy. "It was a grand passion that never should have turned to love. Never."

"But it did."

"That doesn't mean we have to compound the mistake."

"I don't want to keep waiting." He raised his head so he could look at her. "We are missing too much."

"I lost my head over you once; I won't do it again. My future is too important. I have two to think about now."

He took her hands. "Let me care for you, Elizabeth. Let me love you." He turned her hands over and kissed her palms. "I will never hurt you; I will never desert you," he whispered. "Trust me."

Hawk gently reached up and pressed his hand against her lips.

"Don't worry, Elizabeth. Everything is going to be all right."

Suddenly the entire fabric of Elizabeth's life seemed to come apart. She twisted out of Hawk's reach and planted her fists on her hips. "How can you say that? You're not the one who is pregnant."

"It's my child, Elizabeth. And I will take care of him. I'll take care of both of you."

"I haven't seen you for a week, Hawk."

"I've—"

"Please," she interrupted, holding up her hand.

"I'm not interested in excuses. At least Mark didn't give me excuses."

"Elizabeth . . ." Hawk's voice was dangerous.

The floodgates to her emotions were down, and Elizabeth let her feelings come; all the pain, all the fear, all the uncertainty came boiling to the surface.

"At least he never pretended to want anything except my body. 'Your appetites are as big as mine.' Isn't that what you told me in the beginning?"

"I don't deny that in the beginning we came together because of passion and need."

"And even now when I'm dirty and pregnant and frumpy . . ."

"You're beautiful . . ."

". . . right in the middle of my housecleaning, all you can think about is sex."

"Tell me you don't want me, and I'll go." He caught her face between his hands and tipped it up. "Look into my eyes and deny your passion, Elizabeth."

She closed her eyes to shut out his face. Even so, it was etched on her memory, the eyes dark and piercing, the face as fierce as if he were challenging his most formidable opponent.

"I don't deny it," she whispered. She opened her eyes. "I want you, Hawk. I will always want you. I'm trying to learn to live with that. I can't always be a slave to my passion." Two big tears rolled down her cheeks. "I get pregnant every time I do."

"Elizabeth . . . Elizabeth . . ." Hawk pulled her into his arms and rocked back and forth, murmuring soothing words and gently rubbing her back. "We won't discuss this anymore, my beauty. I'll make you some tea, and you can sit in a rocking chair and watch while I do . . . whatever it is that you want done."

She lifted her head. "I don't need . . ."

"Shhh." He put his hand on her cheeks and brushed away her tears. "I'm staying, Elizabeth." His voice brooked no argument.

Her gloom ended as quickly as it had come. She guessed she'd have to get used to mood swings for the next few months.

"If you think you can stand being around a cranky old pregnant woman."

"You're *my* woman . . . and I love you."

She let that pass. She was in no emotional state to deal with declarations of love.

"All right." She went to the rocking chair and sat down. It *did* feel good.

"Just unhook those things up there at the top . . . that's right. That's very good, Hawk." She couldn't help but laugh at the picture he made, all male, his brow furrowed in concentration at the simple task of taking down curtains. Black Hawk would not be easily domesticated. Although she had to admit that he *was* trying. It gave her cause for consideration.

Hawk stayed all day, helping her around the house. Elizabeth was almost fooled into believing her life could always be safe and simple.

Late that evening they were in the kitchen together, sharing a simple meal with the setting sun gilding the windowpanes.

"Change your mind, Elizabeth."

"Hawk, please . . ."

"I know I promised not to talk about any of this, but I worry about you. I need to be with you, watching over you."

"No. I have my life; you have yours."

"It doesn't have to be that way. Come home with me."

"No."

"Then I'll come here. I'll move my things tonight—"

"Don't." Elizabeth stood up, came around the table, and ran her fingers through his hair. "We've had a lovely day. Let's not spoil it with another argument."

"I'm not going to argue. I'm just going to talk sense."

"We always argue, Hawk." She smiled. "I guess that's because we're so much alike."

"No." He stood up, smiling. Then he leaned over and kissed her softly on the mouth. "You are soft and beautiful, lovely to look at and lovely to touch. We're not alike at all."

After he left, she stood at the window, looking out at the darkness, wishing and hoping and chiding herself for being a foolish dreamer. Hawk was not a simple man. He would always be a modern-day warrior, eagerly awaiting his next battle.

"Oh, Hawk . . . how I wish . . ." Her voice trailed off. She wasn't sure what she wished anymore.

The next day Hawk paid a visit to his brother.

"You're good with women, Steel. Tell me what I'm doing wrong."

"Everything."

"That bad?"

Steel laughed, then sat down beside his older brother and put a hand on his shoulder. "I was just teasing. It was my chance to get back at you for always being in charge and for always being right about everything."

"I'm the oldest. I'm supposed to be in charge."

"Elizabeth is a strong-willed woman. I suspect she's having a hard time dealing with that."

"Why? I'm only making good sense. Why should that be difficult for her to handle?"

"Because she's pregnant, and she's probably very scared."

Hawk stood up and paced around his brother's apartment. "I'll admit to being a little scared myself. What if I lose her, Steel?"

"You won't lose her. Don't you remember? The Chickasaws have never lost a battle since DeSoto?"

After his brother had gone, Steel got into his Chevy and drove to see Elizabeth McCade. If she was surprised to see him, she didn't show it. She held the door open as if he were a favored guest.

"Good afternoon. I suppose I should have called."

She smiled. "The Hawk brothers do have a way of dropping in unexpectedly. I don't think I've thanked you properly for helping save my life."

"Seeing you looking so good is thanks enough."

She had a low, musical laugh. Steel thought he was going to enjoy having her for a sister-in-law.

"Did Hawk send you?" she asked as she escorted him into her den.

"No."

"In that case, do sit down and make yourself comfortable. I'll get some tea."

He selected a comfortable-looking chair. As Elizabeth left the room, he absently ran his hands along the sides of the cushions.

"What the hell?" He came up with a strip of leather thong. It felt like . . . it looked like . . . Steel grinned. It *was* a leather lacing from his brother's shirt. The Hawk was not doing too bad for an old man. Maybe there was hope for this marriage after all.

Elizabeth came back with the tea, and Steel discreetly stuffed the thong back into the cushions. She handed him a teacup, and he settled back in the chair and crossed his long legs.

"Look, Elizabeth, I'm not going to beat around

the bush about why I'm here. Do you love my brother?"

"Yes."

"That's good enough for me." Steel set the fragile teacup aside. "He's strong willed and bullheaded and something of a dictator, but he's also brave and loyal and true. I never thought I'd see the day he would fall in love, but he has. He loves you, Elizabeth, and he wants to marry you. That admission can't have come easy for the Hawk."

"Why?"

"He's not just a man, Elizabeth, he's a legend." Steel leaned forward and told the story of his father. "The Hawk was the firstborn. He heard the stories about our father from the time he was a boy. Somehow he took it upon himself to carry out the legend, to be everything our father had been to the Chickasaw Nation . . . and more." Steel smiled. "I'm not saying that my big brother has never had any women. He was always a lusty soul." Steel grinned. "But I guess you already know that."

"If you weren't such an engaging young man, I'd take offense."

"As long as you don't take it with that big gun you carry."

They laughed together. Steel found it very easy to laugh with his brother's woman. He decided that the Hawk had found a worthy mate.

"I guess all I'm saying, Elizabeth, is that the Hawk will never be what you would call ideal marriage material. But I know he wants you and this baby desperately, and I hope you will give him a chance." Steel grinned. "And if he doesn't work out, there's always me."

"The only promise I can give you is that I will carefully weigh all my options and make a decision I think will be best for everybody."

"I had hoped to go home with you in the backseat of my trusty Chevrolet and present you as a gift to my brother, but I guess your promise will have to do."

Steel stood up, and Elizabeth took his hand. "I *do* love Hawk, and I will never deny him his child."

"He wouldn't let you." He bent down and kissed her cheek. "Good-bye . . . for now."

Hawk came that evening at sunset. Elizabeth was sitting in the swing on her front porch when he rode up on his horse. Backlit by the sun he looked like some magnificent god. She put her hand on her chest, thinking that if hearts could stand still, hers was doing exactly that.

"Hello, Elizabeth." He spoke formally.

"Hawk." His name was all she could say, for now her heart was caught in her throat, making breathing difficult. Involuntarily she pressed her hand over her abdomen. Although it was far too soon to be feeling movement, she actually thought she felt a flutter, as if her baby had recognized his father's voice.

"It's a beautiful Sunday evening, isn't it?" He was still being distantly polite. Elizabeth cocked her head to one side and smiled. "Do you mind if I come calling?"

"Come calling?"

"Courting, I believe they used to call it."

"Don't you think it's a little late for that?"

"I don't want my son to think his father did not pay proper respect to his mother."

"Then . . . won't you dismount and join me in the swing?"

Hawk dismounted, and it was only then that Elizabeth saw the bouquet in his hand. It was Queen Anne's lace and black-eyed Susans, tied with a length of fishing cord. He held the bouquet to her.

"For you."

"Thank you." She put the wildflowers to her face. Never had a bouquet been so beautiful to her, nor so precious.

"They grow by the roadside on my ranch. Both of them remind me of you, the wild daisies with their dark eyes and the Queen Anne's lace with its exotic beauty and tough stem."

She laughed. "Do you think I have a tough stem?"

"A very tough stem." He sat beside her on the swing, close enough so that his thigh touched hers. It felt natural and wonderful and right. Elizabeth wished she were a woman without a past, a virgin enjoying the innocent feelings of first love. But she wasn't. She was pregnant and confused and a little scared about her future.

"Thank you for the flowers, Hawk. I'll cherish them." He took her hand. "Do you think we should be doing that on our first date?" she asked with a smile.

"I'm the bold kind. I believe a little hand-holding is in order." He kissed her hand and held it against his lips for a long time. Elizabeth shivered.

"Cold?" He slid his arm around her shoulders. "Maybe you shouldn't be out in the evening chill in your condition."

"It's not polite to mention my condition on our first date."

"Then I won't." He rested her head on his shoulder, then he set the swing in motion. "This is very pleasant, Elizabeth."

"Hmmm."

"A man could get used to this."

It was a beautiful speech with perfect sentiments . . . just what she wanted to hear. But

Hawk was a master of persuasion. She would have to be careful.

She almost laughed aloud. Hadn't she told herself that the first time? Hadn't she promised herself to be careful the night she had gone to his bed? And look what had happened.

"Not you, Hawk. You could never get used to spending your spare time in a front porch swing."

"What about you, Elizabeth? How do you plan to spend your spare time now?"

"What do you mean?"

He turned so that he was facing her and tipped her face up to his.

"You've pulled the shutters back around yourself." She sucked in an angry breath and tried to pull away. "Be still, Elizabeth. You need to hear this."

"How do you know what I need?" She shoved at his chest, dropping her flowers.

"I've always known what you need, Elizabeth."

"It's always passion with you, isn't it, Hawk? I thought this was going to be a nice, pleasant visit. You even brought flowers. But no. You always turn it into a battle of the sexes."

"I'm no good at this." Hawk kept his hold on her, and his face became fierce. "I was going to give you the flowers and be pleasant and charming and then get on my stallion and leave."

His hands tightened on her shoulders, and a muscle worked in his jaw. "It will always be this way with us. You can't deny the passion any more than I can."

"Oh, yes, I can."

"Why, Elizabeth? Why do you want to?" He leaned over so that his lips were almost touching hers. "Don't you see? Shutting me out is another way of running. Denying our love is the same as closing all the shutters in your house and becoming a recluse. You're doing the same thing you did seven years ago."

"How dare you—"

"I won't let you become a recluse from love . . ." His mouth slammed down on hers.

She fought against him for all of two seconds, and then the magic that always claimed her when she was near Hawk took over. She wound her arms around his neck and moved as close as she could get. The swing rocked with her movements.

His lips and hands roamed her body, taking her nearer and nearer to the edge. Moaning now, she dug her fingernails into his back.

"No, Hawk . . . oh, please, no."

"Elizabeth, come back to me. You're mine; you'll always be mine. Don't keep denying it."

"I belong to no man." With her last reserves of willpower, she pulled away from him. Dark, sexy, and brooding, he sat on the porch swing watching her. His eyes seemed to pierce her very soul.

She stood up and pressed her hands together over her tummy. "Please leave now."

He got up and very slowly ran his hands through her hair. Her scalp tingled with the heat of his touch.

"I love your hair," he whispered.

They stood that way for a long while, with his hands in her hair and hers clasped protectively over the tiny miracle that would be their child. Finally he turned and walked away.

She watched as he mounted his horse. Tall and proud in the saddle, he sat looking back at her. She thought he was going to leave without another word. His knees tightened on the stallion's side, and then he spoke.

"You will come to me, Elizabeth. You are mine."

The stallion galloped away, as dark as the night that swallowed them up. Elizabeth sank back onto the swing. Her wildflowers were scattered on the porch floor where she had dropped them.

Silently she bent to pick them up. In the manner of all wildflowers that are taken from their natural habitat, they were already wilted.

Hawk was like his bouquet. Wild and beautiful. He would never survive being taken from his natural habitat—the woods and rolling hills that surrounded him, and the political and environmental battles that cried out for his leadership.

And what about her? Could she survive in his environment? For seven years she had shut herself away from the world. Granted, she had made some changes lately, since Hawk had come into her life. But they weren't major. Hawk was constantly in the limelight. Could she stand that? Would she ever feel safe?

The chilly winds of evening made her shiver. She left her front porch and went inside, carrying her wilted flowers. Upstairs she opened her diary and pressed the flowers between its pages. Hawk's note fluttered to the floor. Was he right? Was she running away again by denying him? Was her past happening all over again after all?

She undressed and climbed into bed, too weary to think about it anymore.

For two days Elizabeth fought against the logic of what Hawk had said. Hawk kept his distance. He was either busy with a new cause or regrouping for another attack on her ever-weakening defenses. She knew him well enough to know that he would never give up on her.

On the third day there was a letter waiting for her when she returned from work. It was postmarked New Haven, Connecticut. Although she hadn't seen the handwriting in a long time—seven

years to be exact—she recognized it immediately.
There was no mistaking the spidery lines and
Gothic curves.

Elizabeth carried the letter into the kitchen and
propped it on the table against the salt and pepper
shakers. Then she made herself a bracing cup of
tea with honey and lemon.

She stared at the letter a long time. Mark Laton.
A voice from her past. Elizabeth was tempted to
throw the letter away without opening it. She had
no desire to know what Mark had to say.

As she reached across the table to add more
honey to her tea, her newly rounded stomach
bumped the table. Her pregnancy would be showing soon.

She thought of Hawk, of the way he looked every
time she refused his advances, every time she sent
him away. Realization came quite suddenly: Mark
was not really a part of her past. He was with her at
this very minute, influencing her to deny the only
man she would ever love, to deny the father of her
child.

Slowly Elizabeth opened the letter and spread it
on the table. "My dearest Elizabeth," it read. How
like Mark to use a term of endearment, after all
these years. He had always been confident of his
ability to persuade her.

Elizabeth forced herself to read on. "I know you
must be shocked to hear from me after all these
years, but I feel a need to rectify the past—if that
can be done. My dear Elizabeth, I treated you
shabbily. Your friend Black Hawk made me see
that."

Hawk, again. Always fighting battles, even for
her. Elizabeth smiled and started reading again.

"You were young and beautiful and innocent,
and I wanted you so badly that I took unfair
advantage of you. I realize that now. Then, I looked

upon our affair as a grand and glorious passion, one that might last through the years. I even pictured keeping you in some small cottage by the seaside, always at my disposal, while I went on with my life as a married man and a respected professor."

"I *did* love you, my dearest Elizabeth. I never told you that. Perhaps I still love you."

"But that's not what I wrote to tell you. I wrote to say, I'm sorry. I'm sorry for deceiving you, for failing to protect you, and most of all for sending you away. The guilt has gnawed at my conscience all these years. I hope you can find it in your heart to forgive me, for I can never forgive myself. As ever, Mark Laton."

Elizabeth folded the letter and slipped it back into its envelope. It was funny how the letter didn't hurt. She felt no pain, no rage, only a vague sadness and an immense sense of relief.

She got up from the table and got a match and a metal dish. Then she held the letter to the flames and watched the ashes fall into the dish.

"Good-bye, Mark." When the last shred of blackened paper fell into the dish, she cooled the ashes with water and put them into the garbage disposal. It made loud gobbling noises as it devoured the last vestige of her past.

Elizabeth gripped the edges of the cabinet and stared down into the sink. Suddenly she felt a wild sense of freedom. It started as a small tingling feeling and grew until it was an outpouring of joy.

"Hawk," she whispered. His name echoed around her quiet kitchen.

She turned and surveyed her surroundings. Darkness made her house appear shuttered. It seemed empty and silent. In rejecting Hawk, she had not created a safe haven for herself, she had created another prison. She felt her shackles fall away as she pictured her future, standing side by side with Hawk, going boldly with him into whatever political or environmental battle he chose to fight, sharing the risks and the danger, sharing the victories and the joy. Hawk had never been the one who needed to change; it was she. And at last she could, for she was free.

Elizabeth turned and marched upstairs. There was no need to hurry. She knew exactly what she was doing to do, exactly where she was going to go.

Hawk was in the barn when he heard the car. He left his watch beside the mare and her newborn foal and slipped outside under cover of darkness. As always, he was cautious, especially now, especially since he was going to have a child. He didn't want his son growing up fatherless.

He saw her coming toward the barn, her bearing proud and tall and the moonlight shining on her dark hair. Elizabeth's hair was loose and swung with every step.

Hawk had to make himself keep from running to her. Their last encounter had been a disaster. He had been determined to give her some breathing room, some time to think. He didn't dare give in to impulse now.

When she was almost at the barn, she hesitated. The moon caught her full in the face, so that she seemed to be glowing from inside. Hawk ached with need for her.

"Hawk?" she called softly. "Are you there?"

"Yes, Elizabeth." He stepped out of the shadows. "I'm here."

"I stopped by your cabin. No one answered the door."

He stood still, waiting. She came a step closer.

"I saw the light in the barn . . . and I thought you might be here."

"Yes. My mare, White Star, has just foaled." The light from the lantern shone on the mare and her spindly-legged foal. The newborn was black except for a white star on his forehead. "The colt will be a fine stallion, just like his sire. He will be my gift to my son."

"Hawk . . ." Elizabeth took one more step, then hesitated. "Once long ago I came to you."

"In the summer, when the trees were green." He held his feelings on a tight leash, watching her, wanting her.

"I came to your bed, Hawk, and together we soared." She moved one step closer, her hand lightly touching her abdomen. "We made a miracle together."

"My son."

Elizabeth stood for a long while with moonlight on her face and the night wind in her hair. And then she smiled.

"You claimed me and said I was yours."

"Yes."

She came to him then and took both his hands. She placed them over her breasts, which were ripe and full.

"Tonight I will lie with you, Hawk, and you will be mine . . . forever."

Hawk swept her into his arms and carried her into the barn. Inside, he set her on her feet and closed the barn door. When he turned back, Elizabeth was standing in a shaft of moonlight.

"I'm free, Hawk, free of the past, free to embrace my future with you—whatever that future might be."

"I will keep you safe."

"I don't want to be safe anymore. I want to be wild and wicked and bold. I want to stand by your side in all things." She reached up and slowly began to unbutton her blouse. "I want to be yours, Hawk, your woman, your wife." She dropped the blouse onto the hay and began to unfasten her skirt. Her movements were slow and sensuous.

Smiling, Hawk leaned against the barn door to watch. Elizabeth had come to him; she had come to claim him. He had all the time in the world— now and forever.

Her clothing fell away, piece by piece until she was standing before him in white silk so sheer, she seemed to be floating. She shrugged one shoulder and her strap slid downward. One dusky rose nipple came into view. He smiled and started advancing.

She shrugged once more and bared her other breast. Hawk reached for her then, bracketing her face and sliding his hands into her hair, lifting it high off her neck. With his eyes gleaming, he let the silky strands drift downward like a dark waterfall.

"For me, Elizabeth, you will always wear your hair unpinned."

"For you," she whispered.

He ran his hands slowly down her body. "You are ripe with my child."

"*Our* child."

"He will be the first of many, Elizabeth." Hawk leaned over her and trailed his tongue down the side of her throat to her right breast.

Elizabeth tangled her hands into his hair and pulled him close. Taking her deep into his mouth, Hawk groaned. The mare nickered softly, and its newborn gave an answering whimper. A mouse, scurrying in the loft overhead, set wisps of hay drifting downward. They fell in a golden shower over the lovers, and the moon washed over them like a benediction.

Hawk lowered Elizabeth to the hay. His eyes gleamed as he braced himself on his elbows and gazed down at her.

"You are my captive now."

"And you are mine." She gently touched his cheek.

"I will never let you go."

"I will never want to go."

He shed his clothes and came to her, claiming her once more as his own.

Epilogue

Elizabeth Hawk sat at her desk in her sprawling ranch home. Summer sunlight poured through the skylights and the windows, unhampered by curtains.

She smiled as she sifted through the latest correspondence. The governor of Mississippi wanted to honor her husband for his contribution to the conservation of natural resources in the state. Elizabeth noted the date on her desk calendar. There was an invitation for Hawk to speak to a conference of foresters on the Gulf coast, a request for Elizabeth to address the Tombigbee Bluff Society for Clean Air, an invitation for both of them to appear on the local television talk show to discuss methods of recycling.

Elizabeth wrote a note of acceptance to the Tombigbee Bluff Society for Clean Air, then put the rest of the mail aside to consult with Hawk. She stood up and stretched, then belted her robe tightly and went into the kitchen to check on breakfast.

Her four sons were in the midst of a huge argument about who would be introduced first at the day's activities. Fifteen-year-old Grant seemed to be winning.

"I'm the oldest son," he was telling his brothers between mouthfuls of cereal. "Naturally the mayor is going to call my name first."

Six-year-old Blackie curled his hands into fists and gave his brothers a look that was so like Hawk that Elizabeth had to cover her mouth to keep from laughing out loud.

"My name is the same as Daddy's," he said. "I'll be first."

Michael, eight, and Jonathan, twelve, got into the act. Soon the kitchen was resounding with the noise of strong young male voices, each vying for supremacy and control.

Just like their father, Elizabeth thought, smiling.

"Boys," she said, interrupting them. "I'm going upstairs to get dressed for the ceremonies. Finish your breakfast, then get ready. We don't want to be late. This is your father's special day."

"How come?" Blackie tugged the edge of her robe. "Tell me again about Daddy's special day."

Elizabeth bent over her youngest child, gathering him into her arms. "Your daddy is a very special man who worked hard so that the citizens would have a place they could come to be away from the noise of the city and close to nature." She ruffled his hair. "A long time ago, when you were just a baby, some people in city government wanted to sell the park and build a shoe factory on the land. Hawk worked hard to save the park."

"So did you, Mother," Grant added, pride shining in his eyes. "I remember how hard both of you fought to save the park."

"Tell me about the shoe factory part," Blackie prompted. He had heard the story a dozen times, but he still loved hearing it.

"Hawk realized that our city was growing without a plan, that factories and industries were being built everywhere without regard to the location. Hawk and a group of concerned citizens—"

"You, Mother," Grant added.

"Yes, I was one of them. We devised a plan that would save our park and provide a separate place, an *industrial* park, for plants like the shoe factory and the new furniture factory."

"Tell the green part," Blackie insisted.

"It's called a green belt. Our group got the city to pass a green belt ordinance so that neighborhoods and parks were protected from the commercial part of the city by strips of trees."

"And everybody planted trees." Blackie clapped his hands. "And all the birds and little animals had homes."

"Yes. Everybody planted trees. And today everybody in Tombigbee Bluff will come to the park for the dedication ceremonies. The park will be called Hawk Nature Center, and there will be a big statue of your daddy in the middle."

"Oh his horse?"

"Yes, Blackie. On his horse."

"I like that. Can I climb to the top of the statue and sit with Daddy on the horse?"

"Ask your father."

"You always tell us that." Blackie giggled.

"That's because Black Hawk is the wisest man I know." She patted his head. "Now finish your breakfast."

Elizabeth hurried up the stairs to dress for the ceremonies.

Black Hawk finished his early-morning ride, which doubled as an inspection of his ranch, then tended his stallion and headed toward the house. His eyes shone as they always did when he knew he would be seeing Elizabeth.

He passed by the kitchen to greet his boys, then hurried up the stairs. He could smell his wife's exotic fragrance, drifting down the staircase. If he were lucky, she would be emerging from her bath, damp and shiny and fragrant.

"Elizabeth," he called, pushing open their bedroom door. She was standing beside her dressing table, wearing a blue silk dress and pinning up her hair.

"You're dressed."

She laughed. "You sound disappointed."

"I am." His eyes lit with laughter, and he started toward her. "But I know a way to change that."

"If I weren't such a decadent woman, I might remind you that we'll be late for the ceremonies."

"And I would remind you that I'm the guest of honor and they wouldn't dare start without me." Hawk pulled his wife into his arms and nuzzled her cheek. "You smell good."

"And you smell like leather and hay . . . and horseflesh."

He laughed. "Are you complaining."

"Never." She laced her hands behind his neck and pulled him down to her. "Where's Sophie?"

"Still riding." Hawk took her hand and led her to the window. Their firstborn, Sophie Elizabeth Hawk, sixteen and full of the joy of youth, was racing across the pasture on Black Star, the stallion that had been a gift from her father the day she was born. "Look at that seat. Look at the way she handles the stallion."

"She's brave and strong and proud, just like her father."

"She's spirited and beautiful, just like her mother." With his arms around his wife, Hawk watched his firstborn a while longer, pride and love swelling his chest and almost bringing tears to his eyes. Without Sophie's help he might never have won the hand of the woman at his side. If his secret liaison with Elizabeth McCade had not resulted in her pregnancy, they might never have acknowledged their love. If he hadn't fallen into Elizabeth's cellar in the first place . . .

"Hawk, a penny for your thoughts."

Hawk turned from the window and began to move in the direction of the bed. Reaching up, he took the pins from Elizabeth's hair. When it was loose, he gathered it in his hands and watched the sunlight catch the gleaming strands as they drifted through his fingers.

"I was thinking of a secret passageway and a dark cellar, and young woman who faced me with a nickel-plated .44 Magnum with an eight-inch barrel."

"Almost seventeen years ago."

"I love you now more than I loved you then, if that's possible." Hawk reached around her and unzipped her dress. Then he slid it from her shoulders. "I never look at you without wanting you; I never see you without longing to hold you, to touch you, to spill my seed in you."

"It is the same with me. I am still your willing love captive."

"Come, my beauty." He lifted her into his arms, and they left a trail of hairpins all the way to the bed. "I am Hawk. Together we will soar."

"Always, my love. Always."

THE EDITOR'S CORNER

LOVESWEPT sails into autumn with six marvelous romances featuring passionate, independent, and truly remarkable heroines. And you can be sure they each find the wonderful heroes they deserve. With temperatures starting to drop and daylight hours becoming shorter, there's no better time to cuddle up with a LOVESWEPT!

Leading our lineup for October is **IN ANNIE'S EYES** by Billie Green, LOVESWEPT #504. This emotionally powerful story is an example of the author's great skill in touching our hearts. Max Decatur was her first lover and her only love, and marrying him was Anne Seaton's dream come true. But in a moment of confusion and sorrow she left him, believing she stood in the way of his promising career. Now after eleven lonely years he's back in her life, and she's ready to face his anger and furious revenge. Max waited forever to hurt her, but seeing her again ignites long-buried desire. And suddenly nothing matters but rekindling the old flame of passion. . . . An absolute winner!

Linda Cajio comes up with the most unlikely couple—and plenty of laughter—in the utterly enchanting **NIGHT MUSIC**, LOVESWEPT #505. Hilary Rayburn can't turn down Devlin Kitteridge's scheme to bring her grandfather and his matchmaking grandmother together more than sixty years after a broken engagement—even if it means carrying on a charade as lovers. Dev and Hilary have nothing in common but their plan, yet she can't catch her breath when he draws her close and kisses her into sweet oblivion. Dev wants no part of this elegant social butterfly—until he succumbs to her sizzling warmth and vulnerable softness. You'll be thoroughly entertained as these two couples find their way to happy-ever-after.

Many of you might think of that wonderful song "Some Enchanted Evening" when you read the opening scenes of **TO GIVE A HEART WINGS** by Mary Kay McComas, LOVESWEPT #506. For it is across a crowded room that Colt McKinnon first spots Hannah Alexander, and right away he knows he must claim her. When he takes her hand to dance and feels her body cleave to his with electric satisfaction, this daredevil racer finally believes in love at first sight. But when the music stops Hannah escapes before he can discover her secret pain. How is she to know that he would track her down, determined to possess her and slay her dragons? There's no resisting Colt's strong arms and tender smile, and finally Hannah discovers how wonderful it is to fly on the wings of love.

A vacation in the Caribbean turns into an exciting and passionate adventure in **DATE WITH THE DEVIL** by Olivia Rupprecht, LOVESWEPT #507. When prim and proper Diedre Forsythe is marooned on an island in the Bermuda Triangle with only martial arts master Sterling Jakes for a companion, she thinks she's in trouble. She doesn't expect the thrill of Sterling's survival training or his spellbinding seduction. Finally she throws caution to the wind and surrenders to the risky promise of his intimate caress. He's a man of secrets and shadows, but he's also her destiny, her soulmate. If they're ever rescued from their paradise, would her newfound courage be strong enough to hold him? This is a riveting story written with great sensuality.

The latest from Lori Copeland, **MELANCHOLY BABY**, LOVE-SWEPT #508, will have you sighing for its handsome hell-raiser of a hero. Bud Huntington was the best-looking boy in high school, and the wildest—but now the reckless rebel is the local doctor, and the most gorgeous man Teal Anderson has seen. She wants him as much as ever—and Bud knows it! He understands just how to tease the cool redhead, to stoke the flames of her long-suppressed desire with kisses that demand a lifetime commitment. Teal shook off the dust of her small Missouri hometown for the excitement of a big city years ago, but circumstances forced her to return, and now in Bud's arms she knows she'll never be a melancholy baby again. You'll be enthralled with the way these two confront and solve their problems.

There can't be a more appropriate title than **DANGEROUS PROPOSITION** for Judy Gill's next LOVESWEPT, #509. It's bad enough that widow Liss Tremayne has to drive through a blizzard to get to the cattle ranch she's recently inherited, but she knows when she gets there she'll be sharing the place with a man who doesn't want her around. Still, Liss will dare anything to provide a good life for her two young sons. Kirk Allbright has his own reasons for wishing Liss hasn't invaded his sanctuary: the feminine scent of her hair, the silky feel of her skin, the sensual glow in her dark eyes—all are perilous to a cowboy who finds it hard to trust anyone. But the cold ache in their hearts melts as warm winter nights begin to work their magic. . . . You'll relish every moment in this touching love story.

FANFARE presents four truly spectacular books next month! Don't miss out on **RENDEZVOUS**, the new and fabulous historical novel by bestselling author Amanda Quick: **MIRACLE,** an unforgettable contemporary story of love and the collision of two worlds, from critically acclaimed Deborah Smith: **CIRCLE OF PEARLS,** a thrilling historical by immensely talented Rosalind Laker; and **FOREVER,** by Theresa Weir, a heart-grabbing contemporary romance.

Happy reading!

With warmest wishes,

Nita Taublib

Nita Taublib
Associate Publisher/LOVESWEPT
Publishing Associate/FANFARE

FANFARE SPECIAL OFFER

Be one of the first 100 people to collect 6 FANFARE logos (marked "special offer") and send them in with the completed coupon below. We'll send the first 50 people an autographed copy of Fayrene Preston's THE SWANSEA DESTINY, on sale in September! The second 50 people will receive an autographed copy of Deborah Smith's MIRACLE, on sale in October!

The FANFARE logos you need to collect are in the back of LOVESWEPT books #498 through #503. There is one FANFARE logo in the back of each book.

For a chance to receive an autographed copy of THE SWANSEA DESTINY or MIRACLE, fill in the coupon below (no photocopies or facsimiles allowed), cut it out and send it along with the 6 logos to:

FANFARE Special Offer
Department CK
Bantam Books
666 Fifth Avenue
New York, New York 10103

- - - - - - - - - - - - - - - - - -

Here's my coupon and my 6 logos! If I am one of the first 50 people whose coupon you receive, please send me an autographed copy of THE SWANSEA DESTINY. If I am one of the second 50 people whose coupon you receive, please send me an autographed copy of MIRACLE.

Name _____

Address _____

City/State/Zip _____

Offer open only to residents of the United States, Puerto Rico and Canada. Void where prohibited, taxed or restricted. Allow 6-8 weeks after receipt of coupon for delivery. Bantam Books is not responsible for lost, incomplete or misdirected coupons. If your coupon and logos are not among the first 100 received, we will not be able to send you an autographed copy of either MIRACLE or THE SWANSEA DESTINY. Offer expires September 30, 1991.

Bantam Books   SW 9 - 10/91

A man and a woman who couldn't have been more different -- all it took to bring them together was a...

Miracle
by
Deborah Smith

An unforgettable story of love and the collision of two worlds. From a shanty in the Georgia hills to a television studio in L.A., from the heat and dust of Africa to glittering Paris nights -- with warm, humorous, passionate characters, MIRACLE weaves a spell in which love may be improbable but never impossible.

ON SALE IN OCTOBER 1991

The long-awaited prequel to the "SwanSea Place" LOVESWEPT series.

The SwanSea Destiny

by *Fayrene Preston*

Socialite Arabella Linden was a flamboyant as she was beautiful. When she walked into the ballroom at SwanSea Place leading two snow-white peacocks, Jake Deverell knew the woman was worthy prey. . . . And at the stroke of midnight as the twenties roared into the new year 1929, Jake set out to capture the lovely Arabella, and quickly found he was no longer a man on the prowl — but a man ensnared.

ON SALE IN SEPTEMBER 1991